DRAW A KOLA
W

Hey earthkins!

For the Great Taranauts Contest No. 4, we asked you to pick up your pencils, fire up your imagination, and drawmagine us a murderous opponent that the Taranauts encounter in Shimr.
Its name? The Killer Kolaverobot!
There were so many great entries that it was really hard to choose, but we did, in the end.
Congratulations, all you mastastic drawmaginators!

HERE'S THE COOLEST K-BOT OF 'EM ALL: THE TRIOVEROBOT! ITS DEXTROUS DRAWMAGINATOR AND WINNER OF THE SUPER JACKPOT IS:

Gia Kapoor, 9
Step By Step School
Amritsar

Priya Kuriyan, our very own TaraIllustrator used Gia Kapoor's Kolaverobot for inspiration!

UTTERLY 'BOT-TERLY VILE-ICIOUS!

Our jury picked these ten drawmaginators for the runners-up prizes.

☺ Hunar Vohra, 9, DAV Public School, Amritsar

☺ Sanah Arora, 9, Step by Step School, Amritsar

☺ Ishita Bhardwaj, 11, The Millennium School, Amritsar

☺ Sanobar Shariff, 12, Sacred Heart Matriculation Higher Secondary School, Chennai

☺ Yashovardhan Shetty, 10, Hyderabad Public School, Hyderabad

☺ S. Soorya, 8, Chinmaya Vidyalaya, Chennai

☺ Sonali Gopal, 6, Westwood, Massachusetts, USA

☺ Khushi Suraj, 11, St Michael's Academy, Chennai

☺ Aditi K., 10, National Public School (HSR Layout), Bangalore

☺ Malavika Srinivasan, 11, National Public School (Koramangala), Bangalore

BEST LATE ENTRY

☺ Warren D'Silva, 12, St Stanislaus School, Mumbai

BEST ENTRY FROM AN OLDER EARTHKOS

☺ Janane Yogeshwaran, 20, St Joseph's College of Engineering, Chennai

See all the winning Kolaverobot entries, in full colour, at *www.taranauts.com*

☺ THE SUPER JACKPOT WINNER gets BOOKS WORTH RS 1500 FROM HACHETTE INDIA + A TARANAUTS ZAPWRAP PENDRIVE ☺ ALL WINNERS get gift BOOKS + A TARANAUTS ZAPWRAP PENDRIVE ☺ ALL PARTICIPANTS GET FUN SURPRIZES!

taranauts

THE KEY TO THE
SHIMR
CITRINES

CHASE THE STARS AT

www.taranauts.com

Roopa Pai suspects she has alien blood, for two reasons. One, she loved history in school. And two, although an adult, she mostly reads children's books.

Roopa has won a Children's Book Trust award for science writing. Among her published works are a four-book science series, *Sister Sister* (Pratham Books), and two girl-power books, *Kaliyuga Sita* and *Mechanic Mumtaz* (UNICEF).

When she is not dreaming up plots for her stories, she goes on long solo bicycle rides, and takes children on history and nature walks in Bangalore. You can find her at *www.roopapai.in*.

taranauts
BOOK SIX

THE KEY TO THE
SHIMR
CITRINES

Roopa Pai

Illustrated by Priya Kuriyan

hachette
INDIA

First published in 2012 by Hachette India
(Registered name: Hachette Book Publishing India Pvt. Ltd)
An Hachette UK company
www.hachetteindia.com

1

Text Copyright © 2012 Roopa Pai
Illustrations Copyright © 2012 Priya Kuriyan

ISBN 978-93-5009-348-1

Hachette Book Publishing India Pvt Ltd
4th & 5th Floors, Corporate Centre
Plot No. 94, Sector 44; Gurgaon 122003, India

Typeset in Perpetua 13.5/16
By Eleven Arts, New Delhi

Printed and bound in India
by Manipal Technologies Ltd, Manipal

To a Shwin and a Nish
With love in Treepli K'8

The Trail of the Tale

Eight octons after the wise, brave Shoon Ya became Emperaza of Mithya, Mithya was celebrating with the grandest Octoversary ever. For the first time, the 32 stars of Tara—the supersun with the cool rainbow coloured light—had come down to dance at the celebrations. Until Shaap Azur, Shoon Ya's evil twin, broke out of his prison below the heaving seabed of Dariya and captured all 32 stars in the Silver Spinternet, plunging Mithya into darkness.

The stars could be rescued, but only if the 32 riddles Shaap Azur had hidden on the eight worlds were solved within an octet. Enter sweet-faced Zvala, child of Fire, athletic Zarpa, child of the superserpent Shay Sha, and animal magnet Tufan, child of the Wind—three gifted mithyakins who had been chosen by the Emperaza several octons ago to save Mithya from the Great Crisis.

Under the watchful eye of Shuk Tee, the Emperaza's most trusted advisor, and the guidance of expert

Achmentors Achalmun, Dummaraz, and Twon d'Ung—
the Taranauts began to blossom into brave, strong,
smart heroes.

For their first challenge, the Taranauts travelled to
Shyn. After many exciting adventures, they cracked the
hidden riddles and rescued the Emeralds. An octoll later,
in Lustr's brain-scrambling Mayazaal, they battled flesh-
eating flowers, weeping trees and hostile minimits in the
company of their mysterious new friend Zubremunyun,
before they set the Sapphires free.

In Sparkl, they had to play—and win—four deadly
games to save the Amethysts. In the end, the Taranauts'
winning mix of superskills, razor-sharp intelligence,
and heart, combined with superb teamwork, saw them
through. On to Glo, where, aided by a giant hakibyrd,
teen pop diva Dana Montana, and Tufan's beloved older
brother, Dada, the Taranauts succeeded in outwitting a
traitor to free the Rubies.

In the icy world of Syntilla, helped along by the
chatterbox twins Cha Patti and Cha Mina and a team of
silverbacked kurmoises, they rescued the Silvers when
they fixed the 'crack'd Silver Bell' at the end of a torturous
booby-trapped trail. In the process, they also unmasked
another, most unexpected, traitor.

As the stakes get higher and anxiety grips both Zum
Skar and Xad Yantra, the Taranauts set off on their next
challenge—rescuing the Citrines. But will they be up
to it?

Now read on . . .

Mithyology

Mithya A whole different universe, with eight worlds—Dazl, Glo, Shyn, Shimr, Lustr, Sparkl, Syntilla, Glytr—that bob around in the endless sea of **Dariya**, around the bad-tempered volcano **Kay Laas**. On top of Kay Laas, in the Land of Eternal Taralite, lives Shoon Ya, the Emperaza of Mithya.

Tara The rainbow-coloured supersun of Mithya. Tara is made up of 32 stars—the Emeralds, the Sapphires, the Amethysts, the Rubies, the Citrines, the Silvers, the Turquoises, and the Corals—in 8 iridescent colours.

Taraday A day on Mithya. It is 48 dings long.

Taralite From 1 o'ding to 32 o'ding, the **Upsides** of the eight worlds, where most mithyakos live, stay out of the water and enjoy the cool light of the Tarasuns, the stars of Tara. This part of the Taraday is called Taralite.

Fliptime At 32 o'ding, all the worlds flip over into Dariya. The moment when this happens is called Fliptime.

Taranite From Fliptime until 48 o'ding, the Upsides are turned away from Tara and into Dariya. During this time, they are in darkness, their buildings and vehicles and forests protected with water-repelling force-fields called **Dar-Proofs**.

Downsides The halves of each world that stay in darkness, inside Dariya, for 32 dings each Taraday. These are scary, unexplored places, populated by creatures of the darkness and not-so-nice mithyakos.

Xad Yuntra The secret hideout of Shaap Azur, Emperaza Shoon Ya's evil twin.

Zum Skar The training centre at the Land of Eternal Taralite where the brightest mithyakos hone their skills. The Taranauts are now in training there

Magmalift A magma-powered elevator inside Kay Laas in which mithyakos can zoom up to the Land of Eternal Taralite.

Aquauto An amphibious cab with the ability to travel both on water and on land. **Aqualimos** are the fancier version.

Stellipathy The technique of communicating directly through the mind

Stellikinesis The technique of moving objects by force of will

Stelliportation The technique of getting to another location without physically making the journey

Hovitation The technique of staying in mid-air for several dinglings at a time

One

'Harharazur!'

Ograzur Dusht entered the forbidding Throne Room at Xad Yuntra and bowed nervously. He was not looking forward to this meeting.

Shaap Azur stayed where he was, staring out of the far window at the cold, rocky landscape of the Downside. His fists were clenched, his broad, well-muscled back stiff with barely-controlled fury.

Dinglings ticked by. Dusht waited, shifting from foot to foot. He wished the Master would get it over with quickly—give him a tongue-lashing, listen to his apology, and let him go. But the unnerving silence dragged on.

'It's the *team* I'm stuck with, Master,' he blurted finally, 'A bunch of blundering gadhasses who cannot complete the simplest operation without botching it up. If I had a better . . .'

'Enough, Dusht!' roared Shaap Azur, whirling around. 'You're just as incompetent as the rest of them! All you're full of is excuses—and hot air!'

Dusht stopped as if he had been slapped. A surge of anger raced through his veins. Quickly, he lowered his eyes and breathed deeply, forcing himself to calm down. It would not do to display such emotions to the Master.

'You want a better team?' spat Shaap Azur. 'Don't whine to me about it—go out there and get one! *You're* the one in charge!'

Dusht raised his head slowly. Surely the Master was jesting! After all, this team had been handpicked by the Master himself, from his closest and most trusted.

'And what of the other Ograzurs, Master?'

Shaap Azur hesitated. Hidim Bi had stood by him for octons and octons, but she hadn't stayed with the game. Her ideas and methods of warfare were from another time, and you simply could not teach an old kukcur new tricks. Raaksh and Shurpa were genius Morphoroops that you could always count on—but Raaksh just wasn't up to it in the intelligence department and Shurpa was too busy defending her brother to come into her own. Paapi was smart, young, a wiz at everything gizmotronic—but too much of an individualist, not enough of a team player. Maybe Dusht was right, maybe the team needed some fresh blood.

'They stay, but you can add others—you're the one in charge, Dusht!' he repeated, more firmly.

Dusht beamed. 'You will not regret your decision, Master!' he promised, trying not to show his glee. All those annoying, supercilious imbeciles would finally get their comeuppance.

'I will recruit a new army from among the ranks of the Demazurs,' continued Dusht, a manic light dancing in his eyes. 'Efficient, capable mithyakas who will not question my authority, who will do exactly as they are told. The brats will be finished, the Citrines will never return to Tara, and you will rule Mithya as you deserve to!'

A rare twinge of self-doubt shot through Shaap Azur—had he just created a monster he could not control? In one stroke, he had let loose on Mithya a highly ambitious young Ograzur who did not always follow the rules, and made almost powerless his other Ograzurs—the only Downsiders who could stand up to him. He wished he could ask someone for advice, but with Achmentor Vak, the one sane guiding voice he had known in his life, having left him, that option no longer existed.

Shaap shrugged inwardly. What choice did he have anyway? Twenty Tarasuns had been returned to the skies by—*oh the shame!*—three puny *mithyakins*. He was rapidly losing the respect of the Downsiders. And his carefully selected team had simply not delivered.

He squared his shoulders and shut the doubt away in a dark, secret place in his heart where he had locked away so many others over the octons. Doubts did not serve a leader well. And there were ways to keep Dusht in check.

'I heard something about you using the Manasbloer without my permission,' he said evenly. Dusht froze. How did the Master know? Who had told him? He had thought he had covered his tracks well.

'But,' Shaap continued, 'I dismissed it as a mere rumour. You would *never* do something like that, would you now, Dusht?'

Dusht caught the thinly-veiled menace in Shaap Azur's voice. The Master knew. He shook his head dumbly and left the room.

'Do you even realize what a *rockstar* your Ma is?' mumbled Tufan through a mouthful of moist chocolate galumpie, spattering crumbs everywhere as he spoke. 'Bet she'd win Masterchef Mithya hands down!'

Zvala screwed up her face in disgust. 'Ewwwww! Do. Not. Do. That!'

'What?' Tufan looked genuinely puzzled as he picked up the bowl and began to lick the bits of galumpie still clinging to the sides. 'You don't think she's good?'

Zvala rolled her eyes. 'Never miiind! I would not expect a savage like you to understand. And *no*,' she slapped Tufan's hand away as he reached for his fifth cheese protlee, 'you *cannot* have another one. Ma packed these for *me*!'

'Did not!' protested Tufan. 'She says clearly on this

note that since she knows how much I love her cooking, you are to give half of all the protlees to me and share the other half with Zarpa.'

'She *does*?' Zvala snatched the papyrus roll from Tufan's hands. 'My own mother? Let me see that!'

'And Mithya's biggest sillykoof falls for it again!' said Tufan triumphantly, popping a cheese protlee into his mouth whole.

'You low-down lying lomdox!' Zvala lunged for Tufan as he nimbly leapt off the bed and ran for his life, grinning. Choking with laughter, Zarpa hooked her feet around the bedpost and stretched across the room to the window on the other side, right in Tufan's path. The next instant, Tufan had tripped over her and gone sprawling.

'Heee-yaahhhh!' Zvala leapt over Zarpa and went for Tufan with the rolled papyrus, smacking him hard as he yelled with pain. 'You're my only friend in this treacherous world, Zarpy!'

'And I'm not?' came a merry voice from the door.

'Ms Twon d'Ung!' Zarpa raced to welcome her favourite Achmentor. Then she stopped short, suddenly wary. How could she be sure this wasn't a Morphoroop? Of course, Zum Skar was protected by a safety shield, but a Morphoroop had breached it just two octolls ago. Tufan and Zvala stationed themselves on either side of Zarpa, equally suspicious.

'I know what you're thinking,' Twon d'Ung's voice was grave. 'You can't be too careful. Let me see, how can I prove to you that this is really me?'

'How about we ask you some questions about us that only you would know the answers to?' said Zvala.

'Fair enough,' agreed Twon d'Ung. 'Shoot!'

'Okay, what stinky yuckthoo brand of deo does our friend here prefer?'

'Max Deo!' said Twon d'Ung instantly.

'Too easy,' dismissed Tufan. 'Here's a tougher one— when you met us for the first time, you came up with a secret greeting for us, just the four of us. What was it?'

Twon d'Ung looked baffled for a dingling. 'That was a long time ago,' she said, frowning as she tried to remember it. Then her face lit up. 'Got it! Come on, make a circle with me and do as I do, okay?'

'Clap three times, jump to the right,
Roll your eyes and fly a kite,
Raise your arms—way high, way low
Pull an ugly face, and say HELLO!'

The Taranauts burst out laughing, just like they had all those octolls ago when they had heard it for the first time.

'It *is* really you, Ms Twon d'Ung!' yelled Zarpa happily, throwing herself on the Achmentor. 'No one else could "pull an ugly face" like that!'

Twon d'Ung gathered them all in a big hug. She seemed to have gotten over the hurt of Achmentor Aaq's betrayal, and looked her happy old self again. Her face had lost the pinched, worried look it had worn since he had arrived at Zum Skar, and her eyes shone with their usual warmth and good humour.

'So which world shall it be next? Who will be the lucky ones to feel the power of the super Taranauts?'

The Taranauts shrugged. 'Well, there *are* only three left,' began Zarpa, 'so . . .'

'Eeeeeeeeeee! You're right! Just three left! I hadn't realized!' squealed Zvala.

Tufan shook his head and tapped his forehead significantly. Zvala punched him hard.

Zarpa cleared her throat and fixed her teammates with a look they knew all too well. It was time to get serious.

'Syntilla is the south-western world, so it's only fair that we go the north-eastern one next,' said Zarpa.

'Shimr!' Twon d'Ung looked excited. 'That's Ms Shuk Tee's world!'

'Really?' squealed Zvala again. 'That's mastastic! So we just have to have to *have* to rescue the Citrines! Just for Ms Shuk Tee!'

'Yes, we must,' agreed Zarpa in a small voice. 'Once we get past the "Manic Monsters" . . .'

Zvala blanched. 'Ulp! I had totally forgotten about that bit . . .'

'Where *is* Ms Shuk Tee, anyway?' asked Tufan, changing the subject before Zvala could start hyperventilating. 'She hasn't come by to say hello all octite.'

Twon d'Ung looked uneasy. 'I haven't seen her since last 'nite,' she said. 'She hasn't come out of her room at all. Achmentor Dummaraz says it has never happened before, not in all his octons at Zum Skar . . .'

Zarpa felt her stomach lurch with sudden anxiety. If something bad had happened to Ms Shuk Tee, Mithya was in very big trouble indeed.

Two

The knocking at the door was sharp and insistent. 'Shuk Tee! It's me. You've got to come out now. I command you to!'

Shuk Tee opened her eyes and stood up. She had spent the last eighteen dings sitting cross-legged on the floor, in the centre of the rough six-pointed star she had drawn herself, meditating. She bristled at Shoon Ya's imperious tone, but she could sense the concern that he was trying so hard to hide. She had come to a decision, and she owed the Emperaza an explanation.

As the door slid open, Shoon Ya braced himself, preparing for the worst. He had been worried since he had woken up this morning—Shuk Tee hadn't presented herself at the Throne Room as she usually did, hadn't answered her summoner, hadn't responded to the

messages Achmentor Dummaraz had slipped under her door. Finally, he had decided to come down himself, something he had never done before.

But Shuk Tee looked just the same as usual—calm, unruffled, in control. The first wave of relief that washed over Shoon Ya turned instantly into anger.

'Where *have* you been all octite?' he raged. 'This kind of irresponsible behaviour is completely unacceptable!'

'Emperaza . . .' began Shuk Tee.

'Save the excuses, Shuk Tee! Of course you are entitled to an octite off when you want it, but at least have the courtesy to let me know beforehand!'

'Emperaza . . .' tried Shuk Tee again, more firmly.

'And to choose this octite of all octites to do this! You do know—or has that vital bit of information completely escaped you—that the Taranauts have returned to Zum

Skar this morning, and need the dingplans for their lessons? There are whispers that that lunatic Dusht is out to recruit the worst scum from among the Demazurs to fight us, and you . . . you . . .'

'I am fully aware of everything you have just mentioned, Emperaza,' Shuk Tee's voice was chilly. 'There is plenty more that *you* don't know about—I was almost munfuddled last 'nite!'

Shoon Ya looked aghast. '*What*? But how? There's no one on Mithya that can mess with your mind, *no* one!'

'Not when I am in full control of my faculties, yes. Not when my defences are up. But if I let my heart rule my head, if I allow my emotions to take over, like I did last 'nite,' Shuk Tee looked disgusted with herself, 'I am just as vulnerable as anyone. At least to two others on Mithya . . .'

'Want to tell me about it, Shuk Tee?' The concern was back in Shoon Ya's voice.

'I suppose I must,' sighed Shuk Tee. 'It is best for Mithya that someone else knows. I will, of course, do my best not to let my guard down again, but,' she hesitated, 'the heart, it is sometimes too powerful to control, even for me. And next time, the munfuddler could win.'

Shoon Ya waited.

'Last nite, someone who was once very dear to me got in touch, after more octons that I can remember.'

'It was my brother, wasn't it?' Shoon Ya said sharply. 'You two always got along famously. I've always wondered why you chose to be my lieutenant instead of his.'

Shuk Tee's mouth twitched lightly at the corners.

'If I didn't know better, I'd say you were jealous, Emperaza. But it wasn't Shaap, it was another. My father.'

'You have a father?' Shoon Ya burst out. Then he looked sheepish. 'Well, of *course* you have a father, or you did sometime, at any rate. But,' he looked bewildered, 'I never heard of him, never saw hide nor hair of him. Haven't you always lived here, at the Land of Nevernite, just you and your mother? Until she passed on a couple of octons ago?' Shuk Tee nodded. 'So where did this father suddenly pop up from?'

'Long story,' sighed Shuk Tee. 'I'll give you the short version. My parents parted ways when I was only six octons old. Ma brought me away with her to Kay Laas, changed her name and mine, and built a new life for the two of us here. I missed Dad quite terribly for a bit, and I kept hoping he'd somehow find me—but he seemed to have forgotten me. Several octons later, the year I entered Zum Skar as a student, I met him again. He had just joined, too, as an Achmentor.'

Shoon Ya's eyebrows shot up. 'I know him?'

'Very well,' went on Shuk Tee, passing her hand tiredly over her eyes. 'Mama was so worried that he'd connect with me again, and that I'd go away with him, back to Shimr She needn't have—he never discovered who I was. I hated him—I still do—for never figuring out. Such a brilliant Achmentor, but he never found me, because he just did not care.' She stopped, looking utterly desolate. 'That's when I made a vow to myself that I would never leave Kay Laas, never again go among the mithyakos, building bonds of friendship and love. Maybe it is a bit lonely sometimes, but it's a price I'm willing to pay for protecting myself from pain and hurt.'

'So how did he find you now, last 'nite?' Shoon Ya asked gently.

'As I understand it, someone from Shimr whom Ma had been in touch with leaked it to Shaap that I was Dad's estranged daughter. Shaap must have instantly realized the power of that knowledge.'

Shoon Ya looked at her quizzically.

'Shaap knows how emotions can destroy our defences—he himself has suffered for not being able to control his anger,' explained Shuk Tee. 'If he spilled the beans to Dad, there was a chance that Dad would try to get in touch with me, and in doing so, would trigger in me some powerful emotion—love, hate, anger, sorrow. Whichever it was, it would destroy my defences, and Shaap would get his big opportunity to munfuddle me. And that's what happened—I *allowed* it to happen.'

Shoon Ya looked sceptical. 'That elaborate a plan just to munfuddle you? I think you give Shaap too much credit.'

'I think you give him too little, Emperaza. If Shaap has let Dusht loose on Mithya, it means he is rapidly running out of options. Think about it—if he munfuddles me, I will turn into a blithering idiot, he will be able to control me completely, and whatever I know will be his for the taking!' She shuddered. 'Thank Kay Laas mithyakins cannot be munfuddled!'

'The very reason we chose mithyakins for our Special Star Force in the first place,' agreed Shoon Ya.

There was a long silence. Then Shoon Ya spoke. 'Thank you for sharing your story with me, Shuk Tee,' he said. 'I am here to listen any time you need me.'

Shuk Tee smiled wanly. 'Talking about it will only make me weak. I have to rebuild my defences, keep the enemy out.'

'Are you talking about Shaap? Or your dad?'

'What's the difference?'

'What do you mean?'

'My *beloved* father, Emperaza,' Shuk Tee said bitterly, 'is a traitor to you and to Mithya, one of Shaap's closest and most trusted. I understand Shaap has just thrown him out on his ear, but that doesn't change anything.'

For a moment, Shoon Ya looked baffled. Then his eyes widened in shock as the truth hit home. 'Achmentor Vak!' he said disbelievingly.

Three

'*Oh it kill-kill-kill-kill-kills me / It makes my hey-ud flip / When the Slasher, the Shredder / Lets the guitarele rip . . . Aaowwwwwwwww! Yeah yeah yeahhhhhhh . . .*'

CRASH! The door flew open and two pairs of feet came rushing in. 'STOPPPP!'

Tufan stopped headbanging to the latest Lustr Blasters hit, stripped off his Hummonica, and stowed his imaginary guitarele. Such a high-pitched shriek could only have come from one very annoying person. He turned around slowly to glare at Zvala. 'Stop *what* exactly?'

'Phew!' Zvala wiped her brow exaggeratedly. 'False alarm.'

'What?' said Tufan again, looking suspicious.

'We thought a bekkat was being strangled in here and we came to rescue it!' panted Zvala. 'You really *must* give us some warning when you decide to sing, Tufan.' Zarpa nodded seriously.

'*Har har*! You guys totally kill me with your cuteness,' growled Tufan. 'Now can you please disappear?'

'All right then, *be* that way,' said Zvala primly. 'I came to give you something I thought you'd love, but . . .' She walked away, loudly and deliberately jangling a bunch of keys on a familiar key chain.

Tufan's mouth fell open. 'Hey, hey, I didn't mean . . . I thought . . .' He ran after her. 'Where did you get those, Zvala? Gimme!'

'Not until you come crawling to me on your knees,' Zvala turned around at the door, holding the keys high above her head.

'Fat chance!'

'Fine . . .' shrugged Zvala, when the door burst open again. Zvala went flying, and the keys to Achmentor Aaq's lab slipped from her grasp and skidded across the floor. Tufan grabbed them, yelling triumphantly.

'Are you okay, mithyakin?' Achmentor Dummaraz dropped all the scrolls he was carrying and picked Zvala off the floor, looking very flustered. Zvala nodded, a little shaken. 'Nothing broken, Achmentor.'

'I'm so sorry I barged in like that,' apologized Achmentor Dummaraz guiltily. 'It's just that I'm a little jumpy these days, and I heard a noise from this room, a terrible noise . . . sounded like a . . . like a . . . bekkat being strangled, actually, so . . .'

'*Mfffft!*' Zvala and Zarpa collapsed to the floor, clutching their stomachs and shrieking with laughter. Achmentor Dummaraz hurriedly stepped out of the room, looking a little alarmed. Thoroughly disgusted, Tufan slouched out behind him, the keys stuck deep in his pocket.

It was only when he had turned the corner of the long corridor that the full significance of the keys now in his possession struck him. This octoll was crammed full of lessons as usual, but Ms Shuk Tee had thoughtfully left in the gizmotronics sessions in his dingplan, even though there was no Achmentor. With the keys, he not only had complete access to the most mastastic gizmotronics lab in Mithya, but also enough scheduled time to mess about in it, exploring a super new invention called MISTRI. *Without* those two sillykoofs breathing down his neck!

Tufan grinned. Woohoo, this octoll was going to be the funnest yet!

'Absolute focus!' intoned Achmentor Achalmun. 'Visualize materialize!'

Zarpa focused as hard as she could, 'seeing' in her mind the corridor outside the door of the room in minute detail, willing herself to stelliport into it. If she succeeded in doing this as it was meant to be done, she would travel across time and space, arriving in the corridor without ever *actually* moving from where she was.

Two dinglings ticked by, then three. Nothing. Would she fail like the others had? They were both so much more talented than she was—Zvala with her razor-sharp brain and gift for pyrotechnics, and Tufan with his natural flair for gizmotronics and his instant tornadoes—how could she hope to achieve what they hadn't been able to?

'Positive thought,' boomed Achalmun encouragingly into her head. 'Fear nought.'

Colouring a little, Zarpa thrust the doubts from her mind. The Achmentor was right. So she wasn't star material. But she had always been determined, and persistent, and unafraid of hard work. Pappy always said those were the qualities that won out in the long run.

As always, thinking of her Pappy calmed Zarpa. Sending a prayer up to Shay Sha, she shut her eyes and forced herself to focus once again. The tingling began slowly. She felt it in her extremities first—fingers, toes, nose, ears. It was very slight, like a mild attack of the pins and needles. She focused harder. The tingling spread inwards, fanning out through her arms and legs and chest, and into the pit of her stomach, where it congregated into a thrumming ball of ionergy and went still.

Then, suddenly, with no warning, a high-pitched drone started up inside her head, and her body began to vibrate feverishly. The ball of ionergy unravelled, radiating upwards and outwards from her centre with such intensity that Zarpa thought she must go deaf or burst into a mazillion individual quarkons. Now she was scared——she wanted to make it stop, wanted to cry out to Achalmun, but her scream stayed stuck in her throat. Her eyes wouldn't open and she seemed to have lost all control over her body.

'Ufffff!'

Zarpa gasped in pain and shock. It felt like a lohiron fist had slammed into her solar plexus. She doubled up and rolled over and over on the ground, utterly winded. A few dinglings later, she opened her eyes cautiously. She was exhausted, but . . . but . . . she had done it! She was in the corridor! A yell of jubilation rose to her lips, and died suddenly as her brain kicked in.

Wait, it cautioned. *Why is it so dark here?*

Zarpa looked around slowly. With twenty Tarasuns back in the sky, the Land of Nevernite, and the rooms and passages of Zum Skar, were now reasonably well-lit. This one wasn't——far from it. Also, where were the arcalamps? Here, only a few mashaalamps burned weakly, throwing flickering shadows on the rough tantrite walls. The smell of petrosene was overpowering.

Maybe she was just disoriented, or dreaming. Zarpa closed her eyes tight and opened them again. Nothing had changed. She looked around for the door that led to the room where the others were. There was none. Far down the corridor, a different door opened on squeaky hinges, and a blast of freezing air swept past her. Zarpa shivered. Something wasn't right.

She saw the shadows before she heard the footsteps. They were advancing towards her, and she could hear the two mithyakos speaking in low, angry voices. Her blood ran cold. She had to hide, and quickly. She edged close to the wall, concealing herself in the shadows, praying that they would walk past her without noticing.

Brrrrr! Brrrrr! The shadows stopped. One of the mithyakos picked up his summoner. At first, Zarpa only heard the buzz of conversation, then suddenly, the voice became loud and sharp. 'An intruder? In this corridor? Send back-up. We'll find him, whoever he is.'

Zarpa began to shake uncontrollably. Maybe she should stretch herself along the floor or right up to the ceiling, make herself so thin that no security system could detect her. But there was nothing to lock her feet around. She should get help, quickly. She sent out mindchat requests to Zvala and Tufan, praying that they would accept. But there was no answering ping.

The mithyakos had switched on their portalamps now, and were racing down the corridor, shining them into every nook and cranny. They were almost upon her hiding place!

'Give me your hand, Zarpa,' Zub's calm, firm voice spoke directly into her head. Zarpa whirled, startled. Zub was standing beside her, his face grim. Zarpa hesitated. Was this a trick? How in Kay

Laas had Zub appeared beside her? But what choice did she have?

She put her small hand into Zub's large one and felt instantly safer. 'Visualize the Tower Room at Zum Skar,' stellipathed Zub. '"See" the Tarasuns! *This is vital!*'

Zarpa closed her eyes and focused. She saw the familiar Tower Room where, every second octoll since the Octoversary, the Taranauts had received their dingplans from Ms Shuk Tee. She saw the Emeralds shining through the northern window and the Sapphires lighting up the southern sky, and the Amethysts and the Rubies and the Silvers all pouring cool, shining Taralite into it. She saw . . .

'Thank Kay Laas!'

The moment she heard Shuk Tee's voice, Zarpa knew she was safe. She opened her eyes, saw Zvala and Tufan's worried faces, saw them rushing towards her. She wanted to smile, tell them she was okay, but her head was spinning and her legs seemed to have turned to wobblejel. The last thing she remembered was a pair of strong arms catching her as she fell.

33

Four

'What actually *happened* back there? Where did I go?' Zarpa leaned back against the pillows of her bed in the Getwellateria, slurping up large spoonfuls of nourishing plumato-flavoured dalbroth. She had slept for 32 dings straight, and was almost feeling herself again.

'Xad Yuntra,' replied Zvala, her eyes wide with fear. 'Shaap Azur's citadel, somewhere on the Downside.'

'*What?!*' Zarpa choked on her dalbroth. '*How?*'

'So here's the thing,' explained Zvala. 'When Shaap Azur took over as Dewanaza of the Downside at Xad Yuntra, he remodelled the fortress and the palace to look exactly like Zum Skar and the Emperaza's palace. It was his way of showing the mithyakos that even though they hadn't chosen *him* to be their Emperaza, he was no less than his twin brother. So when you visualized the corridor outside the room . . .'

'. . . I actually stelliported to *another* corridor that looked exactly the same, except it was somewhere else altogether! That's why Zub insisted I visualize the Tarasuns shining in the sky outside the Tower Room, otherwise I might have stelliported yet again to its mirror image in Xad Yuntra!'

'Zub?' frowned Tufan. 'Where does *he* come into the picture?'

'I keep trying to tell you guys—Zub is *not* to be trusted,' said Zvala triumphantly. '*Every time* we are in trouble, he turns up like a bad pennanna. But does anyone listen to me? *No!* Why? *Who knows?*'

'Are you quite done?' interrupted Tufan. 'If you are, I have a truly brilliant idea. Maybe, just *mayyyyybe*, we can let Zarpa speak?'

Zvala glared but kept silent. Zarpa hid a smile.

'These really scary mithyakos were coming for me down that dark, awful corridor, and I was terrified. Then Zub suddenly appeared next to me and helped me stelliport back. No way I could have done it on my own.' Tufan gave Zvala a withering look. 'In fact, he caught me when I fell in the Tower Room!'

'That wasn't Zub. That was Achmentor Achalmun— he had just raced in through the door,' said Tufan. 'Oh, you should have seen him when he didn't find you in the corridor after you disappeared from the classroom.

He—and his tattoo, I might add—went completely nuts.'

Zvala chuckled, remembering. 'It was pretty funny, actually, now that I think of it—he lifted his robes up to his hairy knees— who has hairy *knees?!*—shouted to us to head for the Tower Room, and ran for Ms Shuk Tee, just *ran*.'

'You *would* notice his knees,' Tufan shook his head in disgust. 'Not how concerned he was about Zarpa.'

'No surprises there,' pouted Zvala. 'Zarpa is his favourite—bet he wouldn't have done that for me.'

Tufan struck his head against the bedpost. 'The MeMe Monster Returns! Zvala, why does everything always have to be about *you*?'

'You mean Zub never even came back to the Tower Room?' Zarpa cut in swiftly.

'No,' said Zvala darkly. 'Ho hum—what's new?'

'What did Ms Shuk Tee say through all of this?'

'She came into the Tower Room almost immediately after we did. She explained what might have happened— that you might have stelliported to Xad Yuntra—and that everyone was trying hard to find you.'

'But isn't stelliporting long distances harder than stelliporting short ones? How did I travel so far on my first attempt, all by myself? It was awful. I felt like I had gone through a stone wall at a hazillion milyards per ding!'

Zvala and Tufan exchanged glances. 'Um . . . we were hoping you wouldn't ask,' said Zvala.

Zarpa crossed her arms and sat up straight. 'Let me have

it. It was something I did wrong, right?'

'No, sillykoof,' Zvala leaned over and gave Zarpa a tight squeeze. 'It was nothing *you* did, it was something that was done *to* you—you were portjacked.'

Zarpa frowned, not understanding. 'Someone took control of your mind,' explained Tufan. 'Then he or she slightly altered the picture of the corridor—decreased the brightness, altered the texture of the walls, cropped out the doors and replaced them with more wall . . . It was all really subtle, and you were concentrating so hard on the general layout of the corridor that you did not notice the changes.'

'Plus, you obviously have a natural talent for stelliporting—the portjacker must have tried it on the two of us as well, and given up when he realized we weren't going *any*where,' smiled Zvala.

'You think?' Zarpa looked pleased.

'Absolute truth,' said a voice from the door. Zvala and Tufan shot to their feet. 'Spectacular Stelliporter.'

Then he scowled at the others. 'Renewed rigour,' he said sternly. 'Post dinner.' He turned and left the room.

Zvala pulled a rude face at Achalmun's retreating back. Instantly, the swirling tattoo slid to the back of his head and pulled a ruder one right back.

'Wish you could come with us, Ms Shuk Tee,' said Zvala. The Taranauts were in the Tower Room, receiving their final instructions before they set out for Shimr the next octite. 'Bet you know your home world so well you can help us find and crack all the riddles in a dingling!'

The corners of Shuk Tee's mouth twitched a little, but her eyes were sad. 'I cannot ever leave Kay Laas, Taranauts.' The three small faces looking up at her frowned in puzzlement, their expressions so identical that Shuk Tee wanted to laugh out loud and hold them close. But she couldn't, she shouldn't. Ever. No good came out of getting attached to anyone.

'Honestly, I wouldn't be much help at all,' she went on quickly. 'I left Shimr when I was only six octons old, and I haven't ever returned. But you do know a little about it, don't you? You must have studied it in mithyography.'

Zvala, help! stellipathed Zarpa.

Mithyography is my absolute worst subject, Zvala returned frantically, racking her brains. *There was something about the Citrines, though . . .*

Think, hot shot! urged Tufan.

Hot! That's it! The Citrines are hot! 'Yes, we did, Ms Shuk Tee,' said Zvala smoothly. 'In absolute contrast to the Silvers, which are the coolest, the Citrines are the hottest and brightest group of Tarasuns. This makes the surface of Shimr an uncomfortably warm place to live. That is why, many hazillion octons ago, the Shimrkos moved underground.'

'That's right,' nodded Shuk Tee. 'I have some grand memories of Oop R'Ville, the Upside's three-tiered underground metropolis.'

'Three-tiered?'

'Yes,' said Shuk Tee. 'Oop R'Ville is designed somewhat like an upside-down wedding cake. Three levels deep—Chuk R'Vue 1, 2, and 3—each level a circle.'

Zvala shuddered involuntarily. 'It must get really creepy as you go deeper . . .'

'Well,' said Shuk Tee. 'A lot of Oop R'Ville *is* dark, and muggy, and . . .' she hesitated, 'yes, damp and fusty, and Chuk R'Vue 3 can be pretty bad, which is why very few mithyakos from the other worlds ever visit, preferring their own cool, airy, Taralite-filled worlds. But,' her head went up proudly, 'for us Shimrkos, it is our land, our home, and we love it.' She paused, a faraway look in her eyes. 'At least that was how it *used* to be . . .

'But,' said Tufan, frowning, 'that must mean the

Shimrkos have been the least affected by the Great Crisis. They are *used* to living without Taralite.'

'Oh no, the Shimrkos are able to bear the darkness only because of the Litechowks.'

'The Litechowks?' chorused the Taranauts.

'The bright, cheerful spaces where the warm golden glow of the Citrines pours in through lofty skylights, the hubs where the Shimrkos come together each octite to eat . . . and shop . . . and celebrate.'

She paused, remembering. Her expression softened. 'Litechowk Aurum in Chuk R'Vue 1 was *the* place for birthversary parties—the best cloud-candy kiosks and shimrlato parlours in all of Mithya, delis packed with honeymallow spungees with golden solaberry frosting, hot buttery creposas stuffed with spicy spudaloo sizzling on street-side griddles, little mithyakins riding on their fathers' shoulders . . .' Her voice trailed off.

The Taranauts stared. Ms Shuk Tee's face was aglow, and she looked octons younger.

'And did *you* celebrate your birthversary there too?'

asked Zarpa, her eyes shining. She would never have dared to ask such a personal question before, but this new Ms Shuk Tee seemed like she would not mind at all.

Shuk Tee started. She looked at Zarpa, blankly. Then her eyes snapped back into focus.

'We're wasting time,' she said sharply. 'The Litechowks have been cold and dark these past few octolls, and they will remain so until the Citrines are rescued.' She glanced at her dingdial and looked sternly at Zarpa. 'Almost fliptime—shouldn't your team be in bed, Captain?'

Zarpa's face fell. 'Yes, Ms Shuk Tee,' she said.

A silent message passed between Zvala and Tufan. They walked up to Zarpa, linked arms with her, and marched out without a backward glance.

Shuk Tee watched them go, heartsick. She had succumbed to emotion again for one unguarded instant, and in trying to pull back, had already caused hurt. She could have, *should* have, shared so much more about Shimr with the Taranauts, all the important things that would help them while they were there. Instead, she had been irresponsible, blathering on about honeymallow spungees and spudaloo stuffing.

She felt a fresh burst of self-loathing. Her weaknesses could end up putting the Taranauts in serious danger. If she didn't succeed in getting her emotions under control soon, she would have to do something drastic.

Five

'*Ta-da!*' Tufan held up three pairs of transparent gloves fashioned from the finest lycrylon on Mithya. They shimmered and glowed with neurowires so fine they were almost invisible.

Sitting on their beds with their backsacks all packed and ready to go, Zarpa and Zvala fidgeted impatiently.

'I think you should pack first, Tufan,' said Zarpa sternly. 'We need to leave in the next ten dinglings.'

'This will take only one,' said Tufan confidently, slipping a pair of gloves on. The shimmering neurowires now looked as if they had been welded right into his skin. From his backsack, Tufan pulled out a short, thin roll of something that looked too smooth to be papyrus and flicked it over the table. It unrolled instantly, and stayed absolutely flat, glowing softly.

Tufan's voice dropped to a deep baritone. 'The iSac,

powered by MISTRI,' he intoned. 'The latest, greatest way of travelling light. Batteries not included. Terms and conditions apply.'

'Your clothes are all over the floor!' said Zvala. 'Shouldn't you at least put all your stuff together somewhere first?'

Tufan smiled superiorly and sashayed towards her on imaginary high heels. 'That's *so*, like, *last octoll*,' he said, batting his eyelashes. Zvala rolled her eyes.

The next instant, Tufan had morphed from Dana Suntana to the Black Avenger. Bringing his thumbs and index fingers together to form a rectangle, he began to 'shoot', pointing the rectangle at everything he could see—the piles of clothes, his Obverse Nanos, a bag of Born-Again Bars, a Hummonica, the crittercaller, and a six-pack of Max Deo. Every time he compressed the rectangle to 'click', the object it was pointing at disappeared, diffusing into a shower of brilliant sparks. The next instant, it appeared inside the iSac, as flat as a freezeframe.

'All done!' Tufan took a bow. 'Except,' he hesitated, 'maybe I should just keep a little something here with me.' Reaching into the iSac with his sheathed fingers, he plucked out a single can of Max deo. It emerged, whole and intact, in his hand.

'That's. Simply. Too. Crazily. Mas.tas.tico!' breathed Zvala. 'May I may I may I?'

Tufan held up his hand. 'One word of warning first. Don't ever, *ever* click at anything that's alive. I know Achmentor Aaq had figured out a way to do it safely, but I haven't a clue!'

'Fine,' Zvala was hardly listening. She grabbed her own iSac from Tufan, slipped on the gloves, and zapped her entire backsack into it with a single click. 'Zarpa, your turn!'

Zarpa picked up her iSac and gloves and slipped them into her backsack. 'I think I'll pack the old-fashioned way for now, thanks,' she said. 'Just in case.'

'As you wish, Captain Worrywart!' shrugged Tufan, slinging on his backsack and running for the door. 'Last one at the Magmalift's a rotten motteg!'

❖

'Well, here we are . . . I think?' said Zarpa doubtfully, stepping out of the unmarked aqualimo onto the deserted pier at Shimr. Zvala stumbled out behind her, followed closely by Tufan. The three of them stood there, mouths agape, eyes bugging.

Before them, as far as they could see, stretched a landscape so bizarre that it seemed to have come straight out of a dream. Gleaming eerily in the faraway Taralite, giant pointy columns of rock rose out of the barren, pockmarked ground, like an army of accusing fingers.

★ ₩ ★

Dense yellow smoke poured out of holes gouged out of the rock and curled tightly around the columns like boasliths, hissing noisily. Between the columns, the ground gathered itself into folds that seemed as soft as protlee dough, falling away occasionally into vast craters or bulging out in enormous, virulent-looking boils.

'Hello-lo-lo!'

The Taranauts jumped. The next instant, they had whirled around, legs apart and arms bent in a defensive Kalarikwon position, ready to take on anything.

A little bent mithyaka stood before them. He was not much bigger than they were themselves. Exactly three long thick bands of hair grew out of the top of his forehead, and were combed down precisely—one was tucked behind the right ear, one behind the left, and the third hung straight down the back. His large head bobbed uncontrollably. His eyes were covered by a huge pair of Tarashades, and half his face was completely taken up by the widest, creepiest grin the Taranauts had ever seen.

'Easy!' grinned the mithyaka, exposing a row of uneven yellow teeth. 'I'm a friend-end-end.'

He extended a small and knobbly hand. 'Treepli K'8, from Chuk R'Vue 3. Honourable Minister, wardrobe manager, praise-singer, bottle-washer, spittoon-holder, shoe-shiner, picker-upper-after, and random-errand-runner to the Most Honourable Maraza of Shimr-mr-mr.'

Pee-ewww! Zvala crinkled her pretty nose. *Am I imagining it, or does this weird guy really, like, smell?*

Absolute truth, returned Tufan. *Spectacular Stinker-er-er.*

Zvala giggled. Zarpa glared at her teammates.

'Thank you for meeting us, Treepli K'8,' she said. 'Will you take us to the Maraza, please?'

'In ascending order of speed and descending order of time taken, there are three routes to the Palace,' said Treepli. 'Infinite Steepstairs, Long Slipslide, Short Sheerdrop—pick one, please-ease-ease.'

The Taranauts looked at each other.

'Long Slipslide,' they said together.

Treepli looked hugely amused. 'Aisi, you asked for it-it-it!' he said, rubbing his hands and giggling so hard Zvala was scared his head would fall off.

'Aisi?' said Zarpa.

'"As I See It" in Shimrtongue,' snapped Treepli, his grin disappearing. 'Didn't you do any pre-trip reading about this world at all? And where are your bags? All bags go down the Short Sheerdrop-drop-drop.'

'We just have the one, and we will keep our stuff with

us, thanks,' said Zarpa, signalling with her eyes to the others that there was no need to reveal any more.

'That's it?' Treepli peered at them suspiciously. 'You're going to be stuck inside for an octoll at least-least-least.'

Zarpa nodded briefly.

Treepli's face turned a dull red. '*Everyone* has secrets these days,' he muttered. 'Even the Tarabrats-brats-brats.'

The Taranauts exchanged uneasy glances.

'Oh, by the way, forgot the welcome speech,' continued Treepli, leading the way across the surface. 'The rock columns you see are the community chimneys of Oop R'Ville, the hollows in the ground are the ventilation "wells", and these ugly swellings,' he spat on one contemptuously, releasing a thick gob of smelly yellow mucus, 'are the skylights of the posh Litechowks where the la-di-dahs of Chuk R'Vue 1 hang out. And now that their Litechowks are Darkchowks, they suddenly need the services of the Uglies they long ago banished to Chuk R'Vue 3. Guess why-why-why?' He turned to them, his face a mask of rage. 'Why-why-why?'

The Taranauts shrugged nervously. Zvala and Zarpa moved closer together, dislike and fear written all over their faces. For some reason he could not explain, though, Tufan felt no fear of this strange little mithyaka. Treepli's anger was real enough, but watching him, Tufan only felt his heart twist in pity. Treepli reminded him of someone . . . some*thing* . . .

'Because of these,' whispered Treepli, leaning in

and whipping off his Tarashades. Enormous yellow eyes stared coldly at the Taranauts. They shrank back in horror. 'Not a pretty sight, are they?' cackled Treepli into Zvala's face, his strong odour making her gag. 'But live a couple of octons down in Chuk R'Vue 3 and you'll be queuing up for a pair. It's these babies that help us see down there in the deep dark-dark-dark.'

'Inombu,' Treepli went on, flicking his Tarashades back in place, 'that's "It's none of my business", before you ask, but imhaho—"in my honest and humble opinion"—you should know that there are many Shimrkos who aren't exactly thrilled you mithyakins are here. And why should they be? Aisi, you rescue the Citrines and cover yourselves with glory, and what happens to us? We lose our new jobs and back to the deepdark we go, ho-ho-ho.'

The Taranauts looked at each other in alarm. If the Chief Minister to the Maraza of Shimr didn't want the Citrines rescued, who did?

'Long Slipslide,' announced Treepli, his grin back in place. 'Lie down on the luge and strap yourselves in, please. The girlkins take one, the boy and I the other ther-ther.'

Two vehicles that looked like miniature sleds stood by the side of a hollow in the ground, their runners glinting a dull gold. They looked ridiculously small, even for mithyakin riders. Inside the hollow, a steep track dropped off into a bottomless hole.

'*Lie* down?' asked Zvala, her voice quavering a little.

'Absolutely,' giggled Treepli. He leaned in on the Taranauts again, making them recoil. 'Here in Oop R'Ville, we love to play the lying game-game-game.'

The guy is insane, stellipathed Zvala. *And he hates us. I'm not getting in the luge! What if this Slipslide doesn't lead to the palace at all? We only have his word for it.*

I agree, returned Zarpa. *He is probably one of Shaap Azur's Ograzurs or something. I vote for bringing him down, now.*

No, Tufan said slowly, his eyes fixed on Treepli's face. *I don't think he's crazy, or one of Shaap's goons. He's just a little weird, and sad, and angry. He reminds me of a kukcur I once knew, who had been kicked around so much all his life that he'd forgotten how to be nice.*

The girls looked at each other doubtfully.

Trust me, said Tufan. *Zarpa?*

I'm not sure about this at all, sighed Zarpa. *But I will go with your instincts, Tufan.*

Instincts-shminstincts! snapped Zvala. *His says 'Aww, poor sad mithyaka', mine says 'Run from the Humpbacked One!' How do you know which one's right?*

Don't even go there, or I will be forced to remind you of a recent incident at

Syntilla involving a certain Lake Shawksar Ovar, said Tufan scathingly.

Zvala glared at him. *No one's perfect* .

Zarpa strapped on her helmet. *This discussion is now closed. Let's go.*

Tufan winked at Treepli K'8. 'Aisi, this is going to be superfun, Treepli. Imhaho, now's the time for you to stick your earplugs in—there's one girlkin right there who can really shriek.'

Treepli's manic grin faltered. The mithyakin was actually being friendly. He giggled weakly.

Treepli pushed the girls' luge to the edge of the hollow. He leaned in again to say something, grinning, then drew back a little when he saw their noses pucker. 'Bolo,' he said softly. '"Be on the lookout". It could be a little scary the first time-time-time.' Zvala clutched Zarpa's arm tight and closed her eyes.

Two dinglings later, Treepli and Tufan pushed off from the edge. Their luge bumped into the girls', setting it off. 'H-aaaaaaaa-llllllll-pppppp!' screamed Zvala as the luge shot down the steep dark tunnel at what seemed like a centillion times zipspeed.

'Warned you!' grinned Tufan, sticking his fingers in his ears. 'Here we go-o-o-o-o!'

Six

'Word has just come in from Nee Ch'Ville,' Hidim Bi stood up slowly and painfully, her old legs creaking a little from sitting cross-legged for over three dings, waiting for updates from Shimr. 'The brats have reached the palace.'

At the other end of the War Room, Shurpa turned to her brother. 'Raaksh, let Dusht know. We need our orders.' Raaksh raced from the room.

'Where *is* he, anyway?' frowned Paapi. 'He should have been growling down our necks for the last couple of octites, but I haven't seen him around at all. It's all a bit strange.'

Hidim Bi and Shurpa exchanged worried glances. The same thought had been running through their minds. Each had heard whispers, but had kept it to themselves, hoping they weren't true.

Dusht was out on their streets, said the reports from Shyn and Shimr, Dazl and Glo, surrounded by gangs of young ruffians, the kind of hoodlums that would kill their own grandmothers for two gold pennannas. The gangs waved their weapons and galloped through the streets on their drooling wilderwolves, terrorizing the mithyakis and mithyakins, yelling something that sounded suspiciously like *Harharadusht!*

Footsteps sounded outside the room. The three mithyakis turned as one towards the door, their faces tense.

'I believe my presence was requested here,' Dusht swaggered in, preening. 'Tell me, how can I be of service?'

'Cut it out, Dusht,' snarled Paapi. 'The brats are already at the Palace of Shimr and we need to stop them from going any further.'

'Oh, I don't think you should worry your pretty little head about that,' drawled Dusht. 'They won't. It has all been taken care of.'

'Taken care of?' spat Shurpa. 'By whom? All the delinquents you've rounded up off the streets?'

'We are *all* delinquents here,' sneered Dusht. 'Have you forgotten the Fiery Lands?'

'Shut your mouth, kukcur!' growled Hidim Bi. 'We fight for the Master, and the Master fights for a noble cause! He has been unfairly treated, and he is fighting for justice. You only fight for personal glory. You will bring disgrace upon us all, upon the cause, and upon the Master!'

'The Master wants to *win,* you idiots!' Dusht smacked his palm hard on the table. 'Don't you *see?* That's why he put me in charge! You failed him! *I will not!*' He stormed out of the room.

Hidim Bi turned to the others, her lips set in a thin, grim line. 'Gather your wits, Ograzurs. Gather all that are loyal to you. Two can play at this game. And when we succeed at stopping the brats before Dusht does . . . well,' her face twisted into a horrible smile, 'we shall see who amongst us returns to the Fiery Lands!'

'Yowwwwww! Ow! Ow! Ow!' The luge landed with a thump on the largest bouncepad and shot straight into the air. Then, with great precision, it bounced down the line of smaller bouncepads, until it slowly rocked to a stop at the last one. 'Off! Off!' yelled a Shimrkos who looked a lot like Treepli. 'Luge No. 2 coming through!'

Zvala and Zarpa unstrapped themselves hurriedly and leapt off the luge. And not a moment too soon! Wild whoops of delight filled the long cavern as Tufan's luge came bouncing down the line. 'What a ride!' yelled Tufan, high-fiving Treepli. 'And the bouncepad landing is totally mastastic! You should turn the whole of Shimr into a giant amusement park!'

Treepli took off his Tarashades and stared at Tufan. Any Shimrkos who could get away had already left this accursed world and fled to others, but this strange mithyakin actually seemed to like it here.

'To the Palace,' he said finally, motioning for them to follow him down a long, dank corridor lit by a few dim arcalamps. At the end of the corridor two bent sentries with sour expressions stood guard. As Treepli approached, they moved their stunsabres aside, grunting. 'Here come the Snotty Superbrats,' said one, just loud enough for the Taranauts to hear, 'to ruin our lives.'

Zvala's eyes welled up. *I hate this place*, she stellipathed. *No one wants us here.*

Zarpa linked her arm through Zvala's. She was about to reply when the corridor suddenly widened into a large high room. The air smelt fresh and sweet here, and the dim light of the distant Tarasuns poured in from the enormous skylight, bathing the room in a surreal glow. At the centre of the room was a large steaming tub of water full of aromatic soap bubbles, and in it sat a large and very overweight mithyaka, laden with jewels, singing loudly and tunelessly. A dozen humpbacked midgets clustered around him, scrubbing his back, washing his hair, painting his toenails and offering him bite-sized portions of exotic-looking food, some of which looked alive.

'His Starness the Maraza of Shimr!' announced

Treepli, in a voice that held equal parts rage and shame. 'Your Starness, the Taranauts-auts-auts!'

The Maraza peered short-sightedly at the Taranauts through a complicated-looking pair of Tarashades, all glowing buttons and dials. 'And about time, too!' he said irritably. 'What took you so long? My once-an-octoll bath is just not the same without the Citrines.'

He waved his bejewelled arms about. 'See? It's all so dull and blah without the lite glinting off my crystals. And I'm stuck with wearing these awful things to help me see in the dark,' he shuddered, pointing at his Tarashades. To say nothing of—yuckthoo!—being surrounded by the Smelly Uglies 48/8—so damaging to my sensitive nasal passages! Off you go, and get to work quick-quick now—I want the Citrines back by next bath-time, and that's an order!'

The Taranauts stared in shocked disbelief. 'But, Your Starness . . .' began Zarpa.

'No buts!' said the Maraza, dismissing them with a wave. 'Treepli, take them away and feed them something. Then come right back here—no one knows where my favourite gold-flecked robes are. Find them quick-quick or prepare for a kick on your backside. Or three-three-three.' He hooted with laughter at his own joke. 'Oh, and once I'm done, you can soak in my bathwater if you wish. Might help reduce that stink.'

Treepli stiffened. He turned around and stalked out, the Taranauts following close behind.

'What an obnoxious creature!' sputtered Zvala, the moment they were out of earshot. 'Why do you let him treat you this way? You should quit!'

Treepli gave a short barking laugh. 'And what good would that do, eh? At least this way, my family is fed.' He shook his head. 'They're all the same, everyone up here in Chuk R'Vue 1,1,1.'

He strode on, his angry footsteps ringing against the rock. 'It used to be different a long time ago,' he said, 'when Oop R'Ville was first built. The taller ones among us were allotted living quarters on CRV1, since it had the highest ceilings, and they worked in occupations that needed natural light—reading, writing, exploring, inventing. The medium-sized ones went into CRV2— they became the goldsmiths and the gem-cutters, the traders and the factory owners. The short ones like my people made our homes in CRV3, and worked on

bringing up the great hidden bounty of the land—gold for trade, crystal for jewels, lohiron to build our machines and magnarails-ails-ails.'

'That seems fair, given the circumstances,' said Zarpa. 'Everyone doing what he or she was best suited for.'

'It was, in the beginning,' agreed Treepli. 'My people were given the greatest respect, because it was the wealth we extracted from the land, at great risk to ourselves, that had helped Shimr grow rich. But about twenty octons ago, things began to change—those in CRV1 began to believe they were somehow superior to everyone else. They closed off the Litechowks on CRV1 to the rest of us, poked fun at us in their newspapyruses, did not admit our mithyakins into their fancy schools-ools-ools . . .'

He laughed bitterly. 'That's why we don't want the Great Crisis to end. A few more octolls of this darkness and the CRV1s will stop being so cocky. Then it will be our time to rise up against them, grind them underfoot! All we need is a little more time—but you three . . .' he spat into a corner. 'You're going to ruin everything-ing-ing.'

Tufan stopped, exasperated. "Oh, come on, Treepli," he said. 'If you felt so strongly about it, you could have thrown us down a ventilation shaft or into one of the lohiron furnaces on CRV2 and that would have been the end of that. But you didn't—*why?*'

'Be-*cause* . . .," began Treepli defiantly. Then his shoulders slumped, and all the fight seemed to go out of him. 'Because," he sighed, looking wretched, "in spite of everything, I care about my land, and I know we will all be destroyed if the Citrines do not return. Because I want to see Shaap Azur and his goons return to the Fiery Lands. Because I believe that goodness and fairness will win in the end, and I believe you mithyakins can make it happen. And because,' his voice dropped, 'if I had hurt a single hair on your heads, the one mithyaka on CRV1 that I love and respect would have never forgiven me-me-me.'

The Taranauts exchanged startled glances.

'He has been up since first lite, desperate to meet you,' went on Treepli. 'He says you know someone very dear to him-im-im.'

The same thought went through the three heads. 'Is he a friend of Ms Shuk Tee's?' asked Zarpa eagerly.

Treepli nodded. 'Something like that. He's her father-er-er.'

Seven

Achmentor Vak paced the floor of his small, spare homecave nervously, wishing Treepli would hurry up and arrive, before the effects of the sleeping draught he had mixed into his sentries' food wore off. He was now officially under 'homecave arrest', branded a traitor of the highest order. By rights, he should have been despatched straight to the Fiery Lands, but the Emperaza had decided to be unusually lenient. Vak suspected it was because he still retained some affection for his old Achmentor.

'Achmentor!' Treepli's hiss broke into his reverie. 'Here they are-are-are.'

Vak turned eagerly to the Taranauts. 'What an honour to finally meet the brave mithyakins!'

The Taranauts gaped at him, still in deep shock over Treepli's revelation that Ms Shuk Tee's dad had served as an Ograzur with Shaap Azur himself! That meant he had actually been part of the plots that had been hatched in Xad Yuntra—to destroy the Tarasuns, stop the Taranauts, and send the Emperaza to the Fiery Lands! No wonder Ms Shuk Tee had not breathed a word about him!

In the few dinglings that they had had to digest this information, they had each built up terrifying visions of Ograzur Vak in their heads. But none of them remotely matched this gentle old mithyaka with the sad, wise eyes.

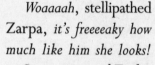

Woaaaah, stellipathed Zarpa, *it's freeeeaky how much like him she looks!*

Ditto, returned Zvala. *Now we know what Ms Shuk Tee is going to look like in, like, a centillion octons from now.*

Assuming, of course, Tufan pointed out reasonably, *that she loses all her hair and grows a long white beard.*

Zarpa glared at her team. Would they *never* get serious? She began to bow to Vak, her automatic response when she was presented to an Achmentor, then stopped herself abruptly. This mithyaka did not deserve any respect.

Vak noticed the gesture, and his old eyes grew even sadder. 'The next time you meet my little girl, tell her I can explain,' he said, his voice breaking. 'Tell her I only ask for a chance to speak.'

The Taranauts did not reply. Vak sighed, then took something out of a bag on the floor.

'We don't have much time,' he said. 'I have something for each of you.'

He handed a comb to Zvala, a spool of metallic ribbon to Zarpa, and a pack of bubblechews to Tufan. 'I know they don't look like much,' he said, 'but sometimes gizmotronics doesn't have all the answers.'

Tufan, whose stomach had been making rude noises for a while, began to crack open the pack. 'Not now, Tufan!' warned the Achmentor. 'Only when it is time.'

'Oh,' Tufan said unhappily, 'but how will I know when it is time, Achmentor?'

Vak did not reply. He seemed frozen to the spot, his eyes fixed sightlessly on the wall behind them. 'Achmentor?'

As the Taranauts and Treepli watched in horror, Vak began to shiver uncontrollably. Before Treepli could catch him, he had fallen to the ground, still shaking, his tongue lolling out of his open mouth. A last, violent shudder passed through his body, and then he was still.

'Water-er-er!' Treepli cried hoarsely, cradling the old mithyaka's head in his lap. Tufan whipped out his aquasip and dribbled a thin stream of water into Vak's mouth.

Vak stirred, groaning. He opened his eyes and sat up.

'Are you all right, Achmentor?' Treepli bent over him.

Vak did not appear to have heard him. He got to his feet and walked with stiff autobot movements to the desk in the corner. He pulled out a roll of papyrus and a scratchscribe and began writing on it, chanting something under his breath.

'By Kay Laas!' whispered Treepli. 'The Achmentor has been munfuddled-dled-dled!'

'Munfuddled?' frowned Tufan.

'His mind is no longer his own—Shaap Azur himself is controlling it-it-it!'

Vak got up from the desk and handed the scroll to Zarpa. Then he stood absolutely still, as if rooted to the ground, chanting the same thing over and over again. 'Eeva nod eeva nod eeva nod . . .'

'Heads together, Taranauts,' said Zarpa grimly. 'I believe we have our first clue has been delivered.'

Sitting on their comfortable beds in their guestcave, the Taranauts peered at the scroll. 'I'm certain the number 1 indicates where to start,' frowned Zvala, 'but the letters don't make sense whether you read them dingdial-wise or anti-dingdial-wise.'

Tufan groaned. 'Stop already! That's the two centillionth time you've said that!'

'I wonder if it is like a maze or something,' said Zarpa. 'Or, or, or,' she said excitedly, 'maybe it is a street plan of

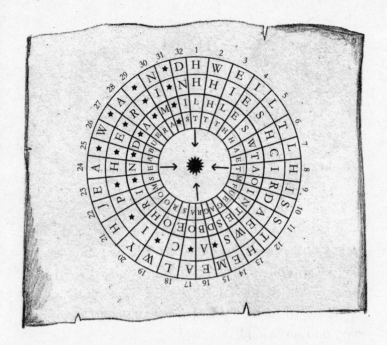

Chuk R'Vue 1, and each letter stands for something—the name of the person who lives there, perhaps.'

'Ohh-*kayyy*,' said Tufan. 'And if it does, so what, exactly? We go around knocking on all their doors yelling "Trick or Treat"?'

Zarpa looked glum. 'Just trying to be helpful . . .'

'Maybe it is a password to unlock something,' said Zvala, 'a password that involves letters *and* numbers . . .'

'Too long,' said Tufan shortly. 'Imhaho, what Achmentor Vak was *chanting* is the missing piece of this whole puzzle, except that it didn't even sound like real words,' said Tufan. 'Just gibberish. 'Eeva nod eeva nod' . . .'

Zvala sat up suddenly. 'Say that again.'

Tufan shrugged. He moved to the edge of the bed, picked up a pair of imaginary drumsticks, and began to play. Drum roll-cymbal, drum roll-cymbal, *drrrrrr-tish!*, *drrrrrr-tish!*. 'Eeva-NOD eeva-NOD eeva-NOD . . .'

'That's it!' cried Zvala, her eyes shining. 'Even-odd, even-odd, even-odd!'

The others stared at her, confused. 'Maybe if we read the even-numbered letters in the circles first and then the odd-numbered letters . . .'

'Oh-kay,' Tufan scratched his chin, 'but do we start with the inner circle or the outer circle?'

'Outer,' said Zarpa. 'The arrows in the centre are pointing *in*, not out. And the first word . . .' she peered at the riddle, 'reading the even-numbered letters from no 2 in the outermost circle, is . . . *With*! It works!'

Zvala began scribbling furiously. Ten dinglings later, she sat back and read eagerly through what she had written. Her face went pale. Mutely, she passed the scroll to Zarpa.

> With steely jaw and hellish maw
> He hides a cipher in his craw
> He waits behind a millstone door
> That fearsome beast — the Muggarosaur!

'In his *craw*?' whispered Zarpa. 'Doesn't craw mean stomach?'

'It d-d-does,' stuttered Tufan. 'I guess that means . . . that means . . . that we will have to rip the monster apart to get our hands on our next puzzle.'

There was a terrified silence. Zvala swallowed hard. 'Before he rips *us* apart, that is.'

Eight

'The Muggarosaur!' shrieked Treepli. A sudden burst of rancid body odour filled the guestcave. 'I thought it only existed in nightmares-ares-ares!'

'Well, this one is obviously real,' said Tufan.

'Go back to your homes, Taranauts!' Treepli was beside himself with terror. The stink was overpowering. 'Shimr will not have the blood of mithyakins on its hands! If the Muggarosaur is about to be unleashed on us, it is our problem, not yours! Go now, go-go-go!' He shoved Tufan towards the door.

'Treepli . . .' began Tufan.

'Don't say a word,' Treepli's head bobbed dangerously at the end of his neck. 'If we had had a better Maraza, he would have found a way to protect you. But you have no friends here—and I, I am only a powerless, ugly midget who's good for nothing-thing-thing . . .'

'Treepli, stop!' Tufan said firmly, shoving him back. 'Listen to me. We,' he pointed, 'we are not ordinary mithyakins. We are Mithya's Special Star Force, the children of the Fire, the Wind and the SuperSerpent. We are the rescuers of 20 Tarasuns, the chosen defenders of Mithya during the Great Crisis.' He pulled himself up to his full skinny height. 'We are the Taranauts,' he declared, 'and *this is our mission*!'

Treepli stopped gabbing. In the silence, Zvala and Zarpa stared open-mouthed at Tufan, making him go red with embarrassment.

Wow—nice speech! stellipathed Zvala finally. *Applause!*

Tufan copped a quick look to see if she was being sarcastic. She wasn't. *Whatever it takes to get the job done*, he shrugged, looking pleased.

At the door, Treepli nodded slowly, and smiled his first real smile in octons. The smell in the cave receded. 'All right, then,' he said, 'you win. But,' his enormous eyes brightened and his grin came back, 'you can't get rid of me so easily. The millstone doors are in Chuk R'Vue 1's maximum security area, and no one but the Hon'ble Spittoon-Holder has the clearance to enter.'

The Taranauts looked at each other in dismay. 'Can the Maraza not approve special clearances for the Taranauts?' asked Zarpa. 'We like to travel alone.'

Treepli looked embarrassed. The stink came back. 'He could, but with this Maraza'—he flushed unhappily—'a clearance could take octolls, and we simply do not have the time. You mithyakins will simply have to make the best of it.' The stench increased.

Oh no! groaned Zvala. *Stuck with the Stinker-er-er.*

'I suppose you're right, Treepli,' said Tufan finally, 'but we will only let you come along on one condition.'

Treepli nodded eagerly. The stink receded. 'Whatever you say-say-say.'

Tufan reached into his backsack and flicked open the iSac. He pulled on his lycrylon gloves and reached in.

Zvala's eyes widened. *Zarpy,* she begged, *tell me it's not what I'm thinking.*

I'm afraid it is, Zarpa sighed exaggeratedly.

Like I always say, Tufan threw them a wicked grin as he tossed Treepli a fresh can of Max Deo, *Whatever it takes to get the job done.*

'Stay close to me!' yelled Treepli, shoving his way determinedly through the noisy crowds at the magnarail station as a mournful whistle sounded from a distant platform. 'And hurry, or we'll never catch the first magnarail to the doors-ores-ores!'

Still groggy from waking up a whole ding before fliptime, the Taranauts pulled their hoodies closer over their heads and scurried behind Treepli down the dark platform as best as they could—bumping into smelly, unwashed bodies and teetering towers of wire-baskets full of mottegs, tripping over boxes, hardcases, backsacks, crates of rapidly spoiling falfroot and sabjitibles, hakibyrd cages, squabbling kukcurs, and the inert bodies of Shimrkos sleeping peacefully through the din. Treepli had insisted on the hoodies, worried that if the Taranauts were recognized, they would be stopped from going further by Shimrkos themselves.

I hate this stupid place! scowled Zvala, extricating herself from the clutches of a bad-tempered Shimrki she had accidentally cannoned into. The Shimrki let loose a string of curses on her head. *How can I avoid obstacles if I can't even see them? Why don't they use more arcalamps?*

Shimr has more arcalamps than any other world, said Zarpa, *because they need them ALL the time down here. But the lamps run on citrionergy, and now that the Citrines have been gone a long time, their reserves are running dangerously low. I was reading all about it in the newspapyrus last 'nite.*

Tufan shook his head. *And they still don't want their Tarasuns to be rescued! Dunderheads!*

CLICK! A powerful freezeframe flash burst into the Taranauts' faces. They staggered back, temporarily blinded. FLASH! FLASH! FLASH! As if on cue, other freezeframes began to go off all over the platform. Shimrkos stopped what they were doing, confused. 'Nee Ch'Ville Attack!' A terrified yell cut across the crowd. Clutching their mithyakins to them, Shimrkos rushed en masse towards the doors. In the melee, a dozen sleeping

bodies rose quietly from different parts of the platform, and began to walk towards the Taranauts.

'Don't just stand there—come on!' Oblivious to the situation on the platform, Treepli waved frantically at the Taranauts from inside a carriage. 'The doors close in less than a dinglin . . .' He stopped, suddenly wary as he noticed the twelve hooded figures walking casually but steadily towards the dazed threesome. 'Taranauts! They're coming for you! Run-run-run!'

Something of the panic in Treepli's voice got through to Zarpa. 'That's us, team!' she yelled, suddenly alert.

'Zvala! Give us some covering fire! Tufan, blow us a path to the magnarail!'

'You got it, Captain!'

Intoning the Chant of Deep Stillness in her head, Zvala turned towards the door of the carriage and stretched her arms straight out in front of her, leaving just enough space between them for a clear straight path into the magnarail. Orange tongues of fire leapt out of her fingers, lighting up the platform.

The hooded figures hesitated, shading their eyes. Zvala aimed at the floor a dozen centinches away. The floor burst into flames.

'Duck!' Zarpa and Tufan crouched instantly. Keeping her fingers pointed at the floor, Zvala moved her arms slowly around to the back, burning a protective circle of dancing flames around her team. 'Go, Tufan!'

Tufan didn't need to be told twice. Planting his feet wide apart, he faced the carriage door, gathered in a giant lungful of muggy air, and exhaled mightily, lifting boxes, crates and mottegs out of the path and straight into the air, where they stayed suspended on his breath. Holding them steady, Tufan whirled, still exhaling.

'Owwww!' Heavy crates and sharp-edged wire baskets crashed into the hooded figures and burst, spattering them with rotting falfruit and motteg slime. 'Get the brats!' one of them shouted as he fell. 'Or I will skin you all alive!' The ones still standing rushed howling towards the Taranauts at their leader's command, unmindful of the ring of fire.

The magnarail gave another mournful whistle, and the doors began to close.

'Grab my hands!' yelled Zarpa. 'Ziggy-zaggy

   7

time!' The next instant, she had taken off at zipspeed, hauling herself and her team through the doors an instant before they shut. The magnarail hovered uncertainly for a dingling, then zoomed away at a terrific speed, hurling the hooded figures trying to climb up to the roof, to the corners of the platform.

'The Superbrats!' Treepli shut and locked the doors of the four-person cabin and flipped open the portholes set high up in the walls, shaking his head in awe. 'The Mastastic Mithyakins-ins-ins!'

'Thanks for the warning, Treepli,' panted Zarpa, as the magnarail sped through the dank, muggy tunnels. 'But who in Kay Laas were those guys?'

A worried frown creased Treepli's scaly forehead. 'I don't know,' he said. 'But I am pretty certain they weren't Shimrkos-kos-kos.'

'Everyone on the platform thought they were Nee Ch'Villians,' said Tufan, spritzing himself.

'They did, did they?' said Treepli darkly, tugging at the single strand of hair behind his right ear. 'Oop R'Villians find it easy to blame Nee Ch'Ville—the mirror image city of Oop R'Ville on Shimr's Downside—for all their troubles, and the Maraza encourages it, so that everyone forgets that he and his chums on CRV1 are really the cause of all of Shimr's problems. No, no—aisi, these thugs were all part of Ograzur Dusht's new army—they may well be holed up in Nee Ch'Ville now-ow-ow . . .'

Zvala clutched at Zvala's arm, her eyes round with fear.

'I think the problem is not who those mithyakas were,' Zarpa smoothly changed the subject. 'We can deal with anyone when we are functioning at our full potential. But we can't *see* anything in the dark!'

'But *I* can-can-can!' put in Treepli, quickly pulling out his can of deo and spraying his armpits generously. Behind his back, Zvala mimed gagging and fainting. *Can't decide which evil odour is worse.* 'So if you have me . . .'

'Yes, but we will *not* have you with us once you get us to the doors, Treepli,' said Zarpa firmly.

Treepli looked crestfallen for a moment. Then he cheered up again. 'Lucky for you I nicked these babies from the Maraza's personal collection, then,' he grinned, holding out three pairs of Tarashades on his long forefinger. 'Your personal Rayviators-tors-tors.' As Tufan made a grab for them, Treepli jumped up and turned off the dim arcalamp in the cabin, plunging it into complete and total darkness.

Tufan groped blindly for the Rayviators. The moment his fingers found them, he whipped them off Treepli's finger, put them on, and gasped. He could 'see' everything in the cabin, but not in any normal way at all. Instead of Zarpa, Zvala and Treepli, he saw bright, multicoloured Zarpa, Zvala and Treepli shapes that moved when they moved. The rest of the cabin was darker—the seats purplish-black with a few yellow patches, the walls a deep flat brown. He flipped up the eyepieces and sneaked a look—the cabin was still in complete darkness, and he could not see a thing. He flipped them down again, and the cabin jumped into life.

Tufan let out a low, long whistle. 'Wayyyyy mastastic! How do they work?'

'I think I know!' cried Zvala. 'They have built-in thermo-seekers that detect body heat! That's why we can see each other so clearly. See those yellow patches on the seats? That's where we were sitting a couple of dinglings ago—so they still retain some of our body heat! And look at me—I'm much, much redder than all of you. That's because I'm Firegirl! Right, Treepli?'

Treepli switched the light back on and shrugged. 'I wouldn't know. Never been to school myself. All I know is that the Maraza had 264 pairs made for him—all different colours—on some other world, when the Citrines disappeared—stupendously expensive they were too.

And he didn't give anyone else a single pair, not even his wife—the selfish so-and-so so!'

'But he didn't reckon with his Picker-Upper-After's nimble fingers and large heart,' said Tufan, slinging his arm around Treepli's shoulders. 'Aisi and imhaho, you are the best, Treepli.' Treepli preened happily.

From the other end of the cabin, Zvala caught Tufan's eye and held it. *Aisi and Imhaho*, she said, *you should stop with the Vechesps and the Vaas already.*

Tufan looked puzzled. *Ve-what and va-what?*

Very Cheesy Speeches and Very Annoying Acronyms, snapped Zvala.

Like, totally, agreed Zarpa, smothering a giggle.

Nine

'Litechowk Central,' Treepli pointed. 'The millstone doors are at the bottom of the crater-er-er.'

The Taranauts looked. Straight ahead was a double-padlocked gate set in a high chain-link fence that stretched away in both directions, circumscribing an enormous circle. Just inside it, the ground sloped sharply into a deep rocky bowl, its rough-hewn surface glinting wickedly where it caught the faint Taralite slanting in through the gigantic dome of Litechowk Central. A narrow gravelly path cut into the sides of the crater led downwards in a loose spiral, overgrown with weeds. There was not a soul about, nor a sound.

Treepli walked up to the gate and unlocked it. 'We will go on our own from here, Treepli,' said Zarpa. 'Thanks for everything.'

Treepli's head bobbed up and down rapidly. 'May Kay Laas protect you-you-you,' he said. Solemnly, the Taranauts shook his knobbly hand. As he turned and walked away, Zvala

felt a sudden wrench, and realized with a shock that at some point over the last two octites, the bent Shimrkos she had found so repulsive at first sight had turned into a friend.

'Okay, let's review the facts before we start,' said Zarpa. 'The millstone doors are the circular stone doors that guard the ancient passages between CRV1 and 2. In the beginning, they were only rolled across the entrances in times of war, to protect the residents of CRV2 and give them time to get prepared while the residents of CRV1 held off the attackers for as long as possible. In times of peace, they were rolled aside, to provide free and full passage to all Shimrkos who wanted to travel between the levels. With me so far?'

Tufan and Zvala nodded. 'However, everything changed a few octons ago. The CRV1s installed guards at the doors, and restricted entry into their tier of

Oop R'Ville. But Shimrkos knew of several secret routes through these passages, and those who had families and friends here managed to regularly smuggle themselves into CRV1. To clamp down on illegal movement, the Maraza

had new entry passages constructed, fitted with more modern surveillance equipment, and the millstone doors were rolled across the entryways for the last time.'

'Got that,' said Zvala. 'I just wish it wasn't so quiet here. It is creeping me out . . .'

GRRRRROAAARRRR! A blood-curdling roar rose from the bowels of the crater and reverberated deafeningly off the sides, shattering the silence. The Taranauts clutched each other in fright.

'Be careful what you wish for,' tried Tufan valiantly, in a weak attempt at humour.

Zvala sank to the ground and burst into tears. 'I don't want to do this!' she sobbed. 'I don't want to be a superkin! I am tired of being brave! I just want to go home to Ma!'

Zarpa and Tufan looked at each other helplessly. Neither was going to admit it, but at that moment, both of them felt exactly the same way. But Mithya and the Emperaza were counting on them—there was no turning back.

Reverse psychology, stellipathed Zarpa. Tufan nodded.

'Tufan,' sighed Zarpa, 'it doesn't look as if poor Zvala is up for this challenge. I propose we leave her here and deal with the Muggarosaur ourselves.'

'I agree,' said Tufan. 'We'll have to survive without Zvala's firepower this time.' He flicked open his iSac and pulled out his Rayviators and his Obverse Nanos. 'Time to go. Set your Nanos to "Grip".'

'Bye, Zvala,' Zarpa pulled on her Nanos. 'Be safe.'

Zvala leapt to her feet, her tears still drying on her cheeks. 'Hello?! Just where do you think you two are waltzing off to? I'm *always* up for *any* challenge. Imhaho—*aaarggghhh*! The Vaas have got me too!—you two could not have survived this far if it hadn't been for me!'

'Well, of all the outrageous . . .' began Tufan indignantly.

'Huddle,' interrupted Zarpa, smiling to herself. The three of them bent forwards in a circle, their arms around each others' shoulders. 'For Ms Shuk Tee!'

'For Ms Shuk Tee!' promised Zvala and Tufan. Then they straightened up, fist-bumped each other, and set off down the path without a backward glance.

'The brats have begun their descent,' Dusht spoke into his summoner. 'Everyone in position?'

The Captain of the Demazurs snapped to attention at the bottom of the crater. His men were stationed in the passages behind seven of the eight millstone doors, ready to take on the Taranauts and the tame shardula they believed was behind the eighth. Only the Captain and the Ograzur knew that what really thrashed and roared there was a vicious mutant reptile with a monster appetite for mithyaka flesh, the result of an experiment gone horribly wrong in one of the top-secret labs on the Downside. 'In position, Ograzur Dusht.'

'You know the drill,' said Dusht tersely. 'And you know what awaits you if you fail.'

The Captain paled a little, but kept his voice steady.

Very few of his men would survive the next couple of dings. As for the Taranauts, his orders were to capture, not injure, but the Captain couldn't care less. Even Dusht knew the Muggarosaur did not understand orders. If something happened to the Taranauts, he could always blame the beast. All the Captain had to worry about now was making sure *he* stayed alive.

'I do, Ograzur,' he said. 'We will not let you down. *Harharadusht!*'

'This is as far as the path goes,' whispered Zarpa. 'The ground is some distance below us. We'll have to jump.'

The three of them jumped off the ledge and moved slowly to the centre of the circle of millstone doors set in the walls of the crater, in a defensive Kalarikwon position, their backs to each other.

Bolo! There's someone there! Zarpa froze as she saw a yellow mithyaka shape emerge from behind a rocky overhang.

'Now!' barked the mithyaka, throwing a lever in the wall. With a grinding, stomach-churning cacophony of stone against stone, the eight millstone doors rolled away. Yelling to give themselves courage, scores of mithyakas came rushing out at the Taranauts, stunsabres drawn, neurozappers at the ready. The light from the portalamps strapped to their heads bounced off the walls, creating confusing patterns of light and shadow.

GRRROOAAARRRRRR! The Demazurs froze. The foul odour of rotting flesh filled the crater.

Zvala whirled in the direction of the sound, and her blood ran cold. Through her Rayviators, she saw a hulking reptilian shape, glowing bright red, crawl slowly out of one of the passages. As she watched, it roared again, rearing up on its hind legs until it towered over them, tall as the Tower Room in Zum Skar. From its massive open jaws, lined with never-ending rows of razor-sharp golden teeth, dripped strings of bright red drool. A drop of it fell on to a Demazur's arm. The Demazur screamed with pain and fell to the ground. Zvala watched in horror as the skin on his arm blistered and crisped.

Step by heavy step, the creature advanced, insane with hunger and thirst. Its head swung from side to side, and its heavy tail lashed out in a wide arc, sweeping up a knot of Demazurs cowering in a corner. The Demazurs flew through the air, shrieking with fear, and crashed to the stone floor a short distance away. With a bellow of triumph, the Muggarosaur dipped its massive head and lunged. The next instant, they had all disappeared into the maw of the beast.

Pandemonium broke out. The braver of the Demazurs turned their neurozappers on the creature, emptying several rounds of tranqslugs into it, but it would not be stopped. The others rushed towards the passages, but the millstone doors had rolled back and there was no escape. 'Grab the brats!' yelled the Captain. 'Get them and the doors will open!'

In one smooth, instinctive motion, Zvala and Tufan pushed Zarpa between them protectively and went to work. *My fire is useless against the Muggarosaur—see how red he looks?* stellipathed Zvala, blasting fire at the Demazurs. *His body temperature is way higher than anything I can produce. Try your luck, Tufan!*

Inhaling mightily, Tufan let fly the most powerful blast of wind he could produce. It spun through the crater at a hazillion anemoknots, lifting everything in its path. A dingling later, carrying with it Demazurs, stunsabres

and loose boulders, it crashed into the Muggarosaur. The monster teetered for an instant, but only for an instant. Tufan gasped. *My tornadoes haven't the slightest effect on it! We have to try something else!*

I'm going for its craw! stellipathed Zarpa. Tufan looked around him. Zarpa was against the far wall of the crater, her feet locked around a ledge. Focusing hard on the Muggarosaur, she threw herself forward and wrapped herself around the vast girth of the creature—once, twice, squeezing tight. The Muggarosaur made a choking sound, slowing down for an instant. Then, roaring with rage, it began to fill its lungs. As its chest inflated, Zarpa lost her grip on the creature and snapped back to the ledge, where she crashed into the wall and collapsed in a heap on her backsack.

Owwwww!

Zarpa! Are you all right?

Yeah, I'm fine. But there's something really big and poky in my backsack that sort of sliced into me just now . . .

Reaching in, she pulled out the spool of metal ribbon Achmentor Vak had given her. It seemed to have grown since she put it in there—it was way longer and wider now than she remembered.

Choking him seems to work! yelled Tufan. *He looked very uncomfortable for a moment there.*

Zarpa nodded, only half-listening. All her attention was on the metal ribbon, which was growing right before her eyes. Suddenly, the realization hit her—the extreme heat radiated by the Muggarosaur was making the metal expand! Now there was enough ribbon to

go around the monster lizard a couple of times. If she could only get it to wrap itself around its middle . . .

Another roar resounded through the abyss. The Muggarosaur had spotted its recent attacker on the ledge and was lurching heavily and angrily towards her, leaving a trail of destruction in its wake.

'Shay Sha! Help me!' Her hands shaking so hard she could hardly hold her end of the ribbon, Zarpa tossed the other end around the advancing Muggarosaur. The ribbon stretched and grew further as it flew through the air, then whipped itself around the monster in two tight coils.

'*Woaaaaaah!*' Zarpa flew off the ledge, still holding on her end of the ribbon. Riding on its momentum, she flew round and round the reptile, wrapping another length of ribbon around him on each pass. Faster and faster flew Zarpa; more and more did the ribbon loop itself around the creature.

Suddenly, the ribbon stopped growing. Through her Rayviators, Zarpa saw the Muggarosaur turn from red to orange and then fade rapidly to a pale yellow. As its body got cooler, the ribbon contracted, squeezing the beast tighter and tighter.

The Muggarosaur's eyes bulged out of its head. Gasping and moaning, it scrabbled desperately for purchase on the stony floor, and failed.

'Tim-berrrrr!' yelled Tufan, grabbing Zvala and racing out of harm's way.

Slowly but surely, the giant reptile keeled over, hitting the ground with a crash that echoed all the way across Dariya to the Land of Nevernite, crushing scores of unlucky Demazurs under its great bulk. Then it raised its gargantuan head for the final time, coughing and wheezing violently. Something flew out of its open, gasping mouth and hit a lever on the far wall. As the millstones began to roll away again, the Muggarosaur gave a last dying sigh and lay still.

'Wait! Get the brats!' screeched the Captain. But the surviving Demazurs were in no mood to listen. Babbling incoherently with fear, they disappeared down the passages, each mithyaka for himself.

Slowly, Zarpa slid off the lizard's back and sank to the ground. Tufan knelt by the Muggarosaur, drawing its eyelids down gently over its vacant eyes. Zvala walked on unsteady legs to where the tightly coiled roll of palmyra lay, glowing a soft red. 'It's still too hot for you guys to touch,' she said, holding it up, 'but here's Riddle No. 2.'

Ten

Shuk Tee sat cross-legged in the exact centre of the Tower Room. She had spent the last couple of dings emptying her mind, so that it was now free to receive thoughtwaves from all over Mithya. She had never allowed herself to worry too much about the Taranauts when they were on their quests, confident that the skills they were equipped with at Zum Skar, combined with their own natural gifts, would be enough to keep them safe. This time, however, since they were in her own home world, she felt personally responsible for their safety.

The mithyakins barely survived the Muggarosaur, someone was saying. *Ninety-six Demazurs weren't so lucky.*

I hear Dusht is recruiting convicts to go after the Taranauts now, someone else spoke. *We will soon have hardened criminals walking free on our streets. The poor mithyakins.*

 86

In the Tower Room, Shuk Tee broke into a cold sweat. The situation appeared to be rapidly getting out of hand.

Why doesn't the Emperaza do something? Or that ice-maiden lieutenant of his? They both sit up there in safety and send mithyakins to do their dirty work for them. Cowards!

It isn't like that, Shuk Tee wanted to protest. It is *easy* for the Emperaza to declare all-out war. But you, whoever you are, do you realize what would happen to Mithya then? We are only trying to prevent the bloodbath, hold it back as long as possible. It is for the greater good!

But this time, somehow, the argument did not bring her the comfort it usually did. What if she was seeing it all wrong? Maybe she *was* a coward, convincing herself that she could do more good sitting in the Land of Nevernite instead of going out there and leading the battle from the front. Was the greater good really more important than the safety of the three mithyakins? What if something actually happened to them? Could she live with that?

She was letting her heart rule her head again. It had to stop, and she knew one sure way to make it happen.

Zub, she stellipathed, *Come in, Zub.*

Always at your command, Ms Shuk Tee.

I want you to show yourself to the Taranauts, Zub. Send them somewhere safe, then take over the battle yourself.

I beg your pardon, Ms Shuk Tee, but the Taranauts are doing fine on their own. I will stay close, but I will not interfere.

Zub! Shuk Tee's voice rose in anger. *I command you to do this! I will not be a coward, sending three mithyakins to do my dirty work for me!*

Coward, Ms Shuk Tee? Zub said quietly. *It takes great courage to let another, especially someone dear, do the things you have let the Taranauts do. You have let them make mistakes that you could have helped them avoid. You have let them arrive at decisions on their own—decisions that you could have guided them towards. But most of all, you have let them confront dangers that you could have easily protected them against. You have already given them the greatest gift anyone can give them—belief in themselves.*

But what if they get hurt, Zub? Shuk Tee protested. *They are only mithyakins!*

I think the Taranauts would take offence at being described that way, smiled Zub. *You know and they know that they are special. By letting them discover their own abilities, you are doing your very best by them, and by Mithya—for the future of Mithya lies in the hands of its mithyakins.*

He paused. *I'm sorry, Ms Shuk Tee, but I will not be the one that undoes all the good work you've done, by sending them 'somewhere safe'.*

A comforting stillness spread through Shuk Tee. *Thanks, Zub,* sighed Shuk Tee. *I feel much bet . . .* She stopped abruptly as two other voices began to speak into her head.

Give me a chance to explain, dear one, her father's voice pleaded. *I had my reasons for keeping away.*

Ha!—your defences are not all they're cracked up to be, after all! gloated the other one.

I'm here now, and I mean to find the real identity of the one you call Zub. And you can't stop me!

Shuk Tee froze. She didn't want to talk to her father, and she would never let Shaap know Zub's real identity, not while the Great Crisis was still on. But how could she stop Shaap now?

You have caused too much mischief already, Shaap, her father's voice was back in her head, stronger now. *I cannot stop you from harming yourself, sadly, but I will not allow you to hurt my daughter.*

A burst of static exploded inside Shuk Tee's brain. She doubled over, clutching her head in agony as a bolt of excruciating pain shot through her temples. It only lasted a dingling, but it seemed to have drained her of all her energy.

Then a once-beloved voice spoke softly into her head, just as soothingly as it had so many octons ago. *Go to sleep, dear one. The monster's gone now. Daddy's here.*

Some part of her wanted to fight him, punish him for all the sorrow he had caused her, but she was too tired. She would do all that—later. Just now, it felt good to let someone else take charge for a change. Sighing, Shuk Tee curled up on the floor of the Tower Room and fell fast asleep.

'Why would a Muggarosaur eat mithyakas when he can eat honeymallow spungees instead?' mumbled Tufan incredulously, through his sixth sticky mouthful. 'I could live on this stuff forever.'

'I prefer the creposas with spudaloo stuffing myself,' said Zarpa, tucking in heartily. 'We should remember to tell Ms Shuk Tee that the food in Litechowk Aurum is just as good as she remembers.'

'Good thing there are hardly any Shimrkos here though,' Tufan licked his fingers clean. 'Or we'd definitely have been recognized. I'm off to get some Shimrlatos now—what flavours do you guys want?'

'Can you both please stop talking about food?' snapped Zvala, furiously tearing up the papyrus sheet she was working on and adding the pieces to the little pile on the table. 'I'm trying to solve a riddle here.'

'You see why I eat?' Tufan said feelingly to Zarpa. 'Just so I don't turn into Ms Cranky-Pants here.'

'I'm not cranky because I'm hungry!' yelled Zvala, who hadn't had a bite to eat since she had woken up.

'Code Red! Code Red!' announced Tufan. 'Call in the emergency services!' He blew a big breath into Zvala's face, sending her hair and the bits of papyrus flying, and fled the scene before she could come after him.

'*Oooooh!* How I want to punch that boy!' Zvala shook her fist at him. 'Now I've to brush my hair again.' She rooted around in her backsack. '*Tch!* The hairbrush is in the iSac. Never mind, I'll just use Achmentor Vak's comb instead.' She ran the comb through her hair exactly 48 times as Ma had taught her, then laid it down on the table and attacked the puzzle again.

'Zarpy, come and help!'

But Zarpa was staring at the comb, fascinated. 'Did

you see what just happened?' she said excitedly. 'The comb just drew all those scattered little pieces of papyrus to itself!'

'Nothing but static ionergy!' shrugged Zvala. 'When you rub a glass rod with astersilk, or run a comb through your hair several times, the rod and the comb get "charged" and can attract things like papyrus bits to themselves. *Now help me with the puzzle!*'

'All right, all *right*, I'm coming!' Zarpa pulled her chair closer to Zvala's and peered at the puzzle.

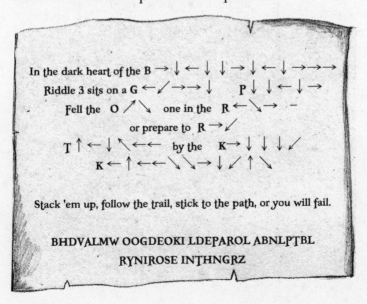

In the dark heart of the B → ↓ ← ↓ ↓ → ↓ ← ↓ → → →
Riddle 3 sits on a G ← ↙ → → ↓   P ↓ ↓ ← ↓ →
Fell the O ↗ ↘ one in the R ← ↘ → –
or prepare to R → ↙
T ↑ ← ↓ ↘ ← ← by the K → ↓ ↓ ↓ ↙
K ← ↑ ← ← ↘ ↘ → ↓ ↙ ↑ ↘

Stack 'em up, follow the trail, stick to the path, or you will fail.

BHDVALMW OOGDEOKI LDEPAROL ABNLPTBL
RYNIROSE INTHNGRZ

'Stack what up?' said Zarpa. 'The arrows?'

'Don't know,' groaned Zvala. 'And what does "follow the trail" mean? There isn't a map or anything.'

'May I?' Tufan snatched the scroll and looked at it for a while, licking his triple-scoop Shimrlato-in-a-cornet. 'Let's try stacking the groups of gibberish words first.'

'Already done that,' sighed Zvala. 'Instead of a line of gibberish, you get a rectangle of gibberish.'

Tufan didn't reply. He put the words down one below the other, stared at them for a long time, then began doing something with the scratchscribe.

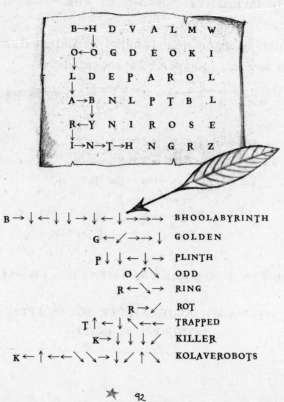

'Shaap Azur's clearly losing his touch,' he said sadly a few dinglings later. 'As is our brainiac over there. I have seldom seen a puzzle so straightforward.'

Zvala looked at him suspiciously. It wasn't possible that Tufan had already solved a puzzle that had lomdoxed her for the last two dings.

'Please don't joke, Tufan,' said Zarpa. 'We really need to get going soon.'

'But I do not jest, my friends,' said Tufan loftily. 'Allow me.' He cleared his throat and began to read.

IN THE DARK HEART OF THE BHOOLABYRINTH
RIDDLE 3 SITS ON A GOLDEN PLINTH
FELL THE ODD ONE IN THE RING – OR PREPARE TO ROT
TRAPPED BY THE KILLER KOLAVEROBOTS.

Zvala's mouth fell open. Tufan pushed her chin up to close it and patted her on the head kindly.

'You already have the first letters of each word. Just find those letters in the grid and "follow the trail" of arrows to the other letters. What could be simpler?' He paused, his eyes round and innocent. 'Or maybe it's just simpler to see the pattern when your stomach isn't growling!'

Eleven

'The Bhoolabyrinth,' Zvala read from her Wikipad, 'is an ancient tantrite fort-maze at the western end of Chuk R'Vue 2, one of the last bastions of Shimr in times of war. Shimrkos guard their knowledge of the heart of the maze obsessively, for the only safe way to reach there is to stelliport in. All that is available to the outside world is the plan of the maze, but the plan hides more than it reveals.'

The three of them stared at the hypnotic diagram.

'Uffpah! It makes my head spin even to just look at it!' Zarpa looked away and blinked rapidly to remove the image from her mind.

'But the route to the centre looks easy enough to follow, doesn't it?' frowned Tufan.

'Yes, but see what it says here. 'The paths inside the

maze are exceedingly narrow, and any creature that steps off the path is instantly paththth'rified, a process that can only be reversed by transporting the paththth'rified object outside the Bhoolabyrinth and chanting over it a secret chant known only to the Shimrkos.' Zvala turned a worried face to her companions.

Tufan was still frowning. 'I don't get it—why can't others stelliport in? Zarpa could easily do it.'

Zvala shook her head. 'Why ever not?' Tufan threw up his hands. 'You just *insist* on being negative!'

'Be-*cause*, genius,' Zvala explained through clenched teeth, 'none of us has any idea what the heart of the Bhoolabyrinth *looks* like! How can we stelliport somewhere that we cannot "see" first?'

'Oh, right,' Tufan looked sheepish. Zarpa thanked her stars that she had kept her mouth shut—she had wanted to ask exactly the same question.

'What does paththth'rified mean, anyway?'

'"Turned to stone",' said Zvala quietly. 'Even assuming we escape that, there are the "Killer K-bots" to worry about, whatever they are.'

'We'll cross that bridge when we come to it,' said Zarpa briskly, standing up and dusting herself off. 'Long Slipslide to Chuk R'Vue 2, anyone?'

'Stop that! I'm running dangerously low on supplies!' snapped Tufan as Zvala grabbed his can of Max Deo and liberally sprayed the air around her.

'This is an emergency, Taranaut Tufan!' croaked Zarpa, snatching the can from Zvala. 'Your captain commands you to surrender a can to the cause.'

The three of them had just stumbled out of the magnarail onto the deserted platform at the end of Chuk R'Vue 2's western line. They had thought the smells at CRV1 were bad, but they hadn't reckoned with what the lack of air circulation a level lower could do to bad odours. It was heavy and musty here, and the stink of dead and rotting things was overpowering.

Zarpa looked around her. No one else seemed to have gotten off at this station, and the magnarail itself seemed eager to zip away into the dark tunnels, back the way it had come. A couple of mangy kukcurs loitering on the decrepit platform set up a cacophony of barking when they saw the Taranauts, but didn't bother to come closer and investigate. From the circular window of a ticket booth a little distance away, a bent old Shimrkos leered at them.

'Headed for the Bhoolabyrinth, are we?' cackled the Shimrkos, flashing them a toothless grin. 'Give my regards to everyone inside. 64 octons at this booth—and I've never had to issue a return ticket!' He cackled again, as if he had never heard anything so funny.

'What does he mean?' said Zvala fearfully as she squeezed herself through the turnstile exit.

'Don't mind him,' dismissed Zarpa. 'Probably gone a little doolally—with loneliness.'

'I see the arrows to the Bhoolabyrinth,' Tufan called back to them. 'They are glowing nice and bright!'

The Taranauts raced down the dark streets of CRV2. The stale heavy air, much lower on oxdrogen than the air on the surface, pressed down on them, leaving them panting and wheezing well before ten dinglings had gone by.

'Slow down,' gasped Tufan, who had fallen behind the others, his lungs feeling the lack of oxdrogen the most. 'Conserve your energy—short breaths . . .'

Zarpa and Zvala glanced back at him worriedly.

'I'm . . . fine,' wheezed Tufan unconvincingly. 'Just . . . a little . . . slow.'

Zvala stared into the darkness ahead. Dimly in the distance, she saw the shape of an entrance arch, and gave a shout of triumph. 'We're almost there, Tufan! Steady, now! The moment we're out of the maze, we'll head straight to a ventilation shaft and fill up with fresh air.'

In response, the Tufan blob gave a weak thumbs-up. 'Don't worry . . . not planning to . . . die on you . . . anytime soon . . .'

Absolute focus! commanded Zarpa as the Taranauts stepped on to the narrow path. A couple of metrinches away on either side, rough tantrite walls rose all the way to the ceiling, gleaming a dull grey-black through the Rayviators. *One foot after another. Stay within the lines.*

My legs are shaking too hard, whispered Zvala. *Don't think I can do this.*

You can, too! snapped Zarpa. *The one we both should be worried about is Tufan! How are you doing back there, Tufan?*

Okay, said Tufan shortly. In reality, he felt exactly like the Muggarosaur must have when Zarpa's ribbon tightened around its chest, but he wasn't about to let Zarpa know that.

Step by unsteady step, the Taranauts progressed down the path. The first circle went off without incident. *We can do this!*

Turning the corner, they entered the outermost circle of the maze. Zarpa paused. Had the path narrowed further or was she imagining it? Maybe she was—Zvala seemed to be doing just fine a little ahead of her. She turned back to check on Tufan. It was difficult to tell for sure, but he seemed to be weakening—his steps didn't seem as sure as Zvala's, and his shoulders slumped.

I think I'm getting the hang of this, began Zvala, *maybe it's easier for mithyakins because our feet are so much smaller, righ …*

The words died in her throat. Straight ahead of her, by the side of the path, stood a large ice-blue mithyaka shape, his neurozapper pointing straight at her! Behind him stood another, his stunsabre raised high above his head.

Behind her, Zarpa gave a sudden nervous giggle. *Chillax, Zvala! They're harmless*, she said, fighting to keep her voice steady. *They're the ones that … didn't make it.*

Zvala sighed with relief. In the absolute quiet of the Bhoolabyrinth, her breath sounded startlingly loud. Then, suddenly, another sound burst upon them, loud and insistent, shattering the silence.

BEEP! BEEP! BEEP! Arcalamps flashed on and off, blinding the girls. Their hearts sinking, Zarpa and Zvala turned slowly around. Sprawled on the side of the path behind them was an ice-blue Tufan shape.

The sight seemed to flip a switch inside Zarpa. The cool-headed captain disappeared, leaving a hysterical mithyakin in her place. 'This is all my fault! I knew he was in trouble even before we got into the maze! I should have insisted he stay outside! Zvala, we have to take Tufan out of the maze now! We must . . .'

The Zarpa blob had turned from a steady yellow-orange to a bright orange-red. A wave of panic swept over Zvala. 'Zarpa! Listen to me,' she said urgently, in as calm a voice as she could manage. 'We have to carry on now. We will take him with us on our way out.'

'No, Zvala, no!' sobbed the Zvala blob, beginning to turn completely red. 'I am your Captain! *You* listen to *me*! If you don't want to help me, I'll take him out myself!'

'Zarpa, nooooooo!'

But Zarpa was too far gone to listen. As Zvala watched in horror, the deafening alarm went off again. In a twinkling, the Zarpa shape turned from bright red to ice blue.

Twelve

For several dinglings, Zvala stood still, intoning the Chant of Deep Stillness. She was more terrified than she had ever been in her life, but somewhere behind the terror was a strange calm, coupled with a steely determination. She was the only Taranaut left standing, and from where she stood, the chances of her making it to the heart of the Bhoolabyrinth were painfully slim. But she did not mean to let Shaap Azur win without a fight.

Absolute focus! she told herself sternly. *One foot after the other—it's that easy.* She would not think about Zarpa and Tufan frozen into stone on the side of the path. She would not think of what an impossible task it was to get *both* of them out, all on her own. She would not think about how she could possibly fight off a ring of Kolaverobots all by herself. She would not think about *anything* but the path in front of her, see nothing but the boundary lines that gleamed a dull brass through the Rayviators.

One step after another, one step after another, endlessly, round and round the winding path. Never stopping to check how much further to go, never pausing to rest her legs—she would not slacken if it took an octon.

Suddenly, as she knew they must sometime, the boundary lines ended. She had made it!

In front of her was a high cavern, large enough to hold at least a hazillion Shimrkos. In its centre, around a pedestal that glowed a soft tawny gold, stood a circle of sixteen identical ice-blue autobots, armed to the teeth, shoulder to shoulder. Their heads were veiled in identical shrouds, their wheels eerily still. A scroll of papyrus rested on the pedestal—Riddle No. 3.

Zvala stepped into the cavern. The next instant, with a grinding and squeaking that set her teeth on edge, a millstone rolled across the entrance to the path she had just arrived by.

'Well, I'm here now,' gulped Zvala, speaking aloud. The absolute silence was getting to her. 'You must be the

Kolaverobots—hello! I must say you don't look half as scary as the Muggarosaur. What next? Ummm . . . how did the riddle go? *Fell the odd one or prepare to rot . . .* But how do I tell which one of you is the odd one out? Would you pull off your veils please?'

The K-bots did not answer.

'What if I felled all of you instead? That would just make everything simpler, wouldn't it?'

She raised her arm and let loose a blast of firepower at the K-bots. The moment the fire touched one of them, the ring of K-bots came alive, roaring with rage, and began to converge on every corner of the cavern, their spinscythe hands slashing murderously through the air!

'Uh-oh, bad move! Sorry, guys!' Zvala ducked and feinted, sending off blistering tongues of flame in every direction. But each time, the fire lasted only a moment before it sputtered and went out. 'What's *with* you, fingers?' yelled Zvala, taking in a giant lungful of stale air and exhaling. A thin blue flame came out of her mouth mouth, struggled in vain to grow into a blaze, and died out.

Fear gripped Zvala as the truth hit her. Fire could not burn without oxdrogen! She was now powerless against the K-bots! Sooner or later, one of those spinscythes would get her—she could not run forever.

The comb, Zvala. Zub's voice boomed into her head.

Achmentor Vak's comb? What can I do with a comb? demanded Zvala, bending backwards to avoid a whirring spinscythe. *Zub, you've got to be more helpful than that.*

There was no answer. Cursing Zub furiously under her

breath, Zvala pulled out the comb and pointed it at the Kolaverobots. Nothing happened. An image of papyrus bits clinging to the comb flashed through her head. Could it be . . .? Ducking and weaving through the bots, Zvala began to comb her hair. Forty-eight strokes, just as Ma had taught her. With each stroke, the comb crackled and sparked with ionergy.

'Done!' yelled Zvala pulling the comb through her hair for the forty-eighth time and pointing it at the K-bots. They did not stop moving, but the shrouds covering their heads flew and moved as one towards the comb, revealing sixteen identical faces. Fifteen were ice-blue, the odd one out glowed an eerie luminescent yellow.

'Gotcha!' Concentrating all her energies into her index finger, Zvala generated a powerful heat beam. The beam slammed into the yellow face, melting it and revealing the complex gizmotronic circuitry inside.

Destroying the 'odd one' had an instant effect on the other K-bots—their engines shut down, and they froze in position. The millstone doors began to roll away.

Racing to the plinth, Zvala plucked off the scroll. 'Now for the long walk back.'

Half a ding later, still running on pure adrenalin and absolute focus, she stood in front of the two pathth'rified figures that used to be her friends. Gingerly, making sure her feet did not overstep the boundary lines, she leaned over and gave the Zarpa shape a push. It did not budge. No question about it—these figures had the weight and density of solid stone, too heavy for her to carry.

Zvala did not despair. Her brain was sparking on all cylinders right now—she was confident she would find a way. She opened her backsack and peered in, looking for inspiration, and found it.

Quickly, she pulled on her MISTRI gloves and flicked open the iSac inside the bag. She remembered Tufan saying that they weren't to click at mithyakos, but these figures were not mithyakos; they were merely *images* of mithyakos. She made a rectangle of her fingers, pointed at each in turn, and 'clicked'. Zarpa and Tufan disappeared in a shower of sparks and reappeared inside the iSac.

'Let's go, team!' Zvala patted her backsack and headed up the path again.

'Quickly, quickly! You mithyakins are running out of time-ime-ime!'

'Treepli?' Zvala peered incredulously at the bent little mithyaka shape standing under what looked like the entrance arch a few metrinches away. She had made it out of the Bhoolabyrinth! Weak with relief, Zvala began to sob uncontrollably.

Treepli's face crumpled in concern. 'What happened, mithyakin? Where are the others? Surely they're not . . . they haven't been . . . pathth'rified-ied-ied?'

Zvala nodded miserably, tears running down her face. 'Well, *don't* you worry about it,' he reassured her hurriedly. 'I'll round up some of my friends, and we'll go in there and bring them out and . . .'

'I have them with me—I hope . . .' whispered Zvala. Treepli looked around and behind her, puzzled. 'Where?'

Zvala flicked open her iSac and pointed. Treepli's big yellow eyes grew bigger and rounder. Zvala sent up a silent prayer, reached in with her gloves, and pulled at Zarpa.

'Woaaaah!' Zvala staggered back under the weight of the Zarpa figure as it popped out of the iSac, whole and intact. Quickly, she reached in again and pulled the Tufan figure out.

'Well-well-well, I'll be-be-be . . .' stuttered Treepli. 'Imhaho, that's just . . . . . . mastastic-tic-tic!'

Zvala still looked worried. 'You think you can . . .?'

'Of course, of course, mithyakin-kin-kin,' Treepli composed himself. He raised his hands above the two figures, closed his eyes, and chanted a stream of gibberish. As Zvala watched, the ice-blue figures began to pulse a warm orange-yellow.

'Eeeeeeeeeeeee!' Zvala jumped on a very surprised Zarpa, knocking her to the ground beside Tufan. She threw her arms around both of them and squeezed hard.

'Eeeee to you too . . .' Tufan protested weakly. 'Can't . . . breathe . . .'

Zvala and Zarpa moved away instantly. 'The nearest ventilation shaft, Treepli!' called Zarpa, grabbing Tufan's arm and preparing to zip. 'Hurry!'

Zarpa, Zvala and Tufan sat around the table in their guestcave in CRV2, digging into mega bowls of Shimrlato

sundaes after polishing off an enormous breakfast. Tufan was feeling almost like himself again after recharging his lungs with a hazillion deep breaths of oxdrogen-rich air. Treepli had finally—and reluctantly—left a few dinglings before, assuring Tufan that as his lungs adapted, like the Shimrkos' lungs, to the low levels of oxdrogen, he would be able to use his powers again.

'I have some bad news,' Zarpa pushed away her empty bowl and looked around at her team. 'What we did not know about the Bhoolabyrinth is that it is a Tymxler8'r.' Two faces stared at her uncomprehendingly.

'Time speeds up when you are inside it,' explained Zarpa. 'We believed we spent about four dings in there. The reality was closer to two *octites*.'

'*What!?*' Zvala jumped to her feet. 'That means we only have until fliptime tomorrow to crack all the riddles!'

Tufan burped loudly and contentedly. '*That* explains why I was so famished,' he beamed, as Zvala gagged. 'Now if you girls will excuse me, I need to pop into the shower for a bit.'

'*No*, Tufan!' said Zarpa. 'You already had a shower last 'nite. You need to be here—we have a riddle to crack!'

'Oh, let him go,' said Zvala hastily, desperate to win back her Brainiac title. 'I'll have this cracked by the time he is out of there.'

'Or *not*,' said Tufan. 'In which case, I'll take a look and solve it in two dinglings, like I usually do.'

'Funn-*ee*!' snapped Zvala. 'Just *go!*' She opened the scroll and smoothed it out on the table.

'Well, that doesn't look too hard—it looks like one of Achalmun's substitution codes.'

Zarpa pinched her lower lip, frowning. 'But those were usually about substituting a number for a letter or a letter for another letter,' she said. 'What's with these funny shapes and stars?'

Zvala stared at the scroll some more. 'I think the way it works is like this,' she said slowly, taking out a scratchscribe and drawing a shape with it. 'This'—she drew └─—'would represent E or F, because that pair of letters is in a "box" that has only two sides, shaped like L. 'And this shape'— she drew ⌐─'would represent either O or P, and this one here'—she made ☐—'I or J', and this one'—she drew ∧—'would be Y or Z, and so on . . . But,' she shook her head, 'I can't figure out what the stars mean.'

'I know!' cried Zarpa. 'The placing of the stars in the grid is not random! Each star is placed directly above a certain letter! So this shape'—she took the scratchscribe from Zvala and drew ∨—'represents the letter S, while this one'—she drew ⩔—'represents the letter T, because that's the letter over which the star is! Right?' She looked at Zvala for approval, eyes shining.

'Suddenly, *everyone's* a genius,' sulked Zvala. 'Of *course* that's how it works. Don't know *how* I didn't figure it out.'

'The same way I didn't figure out how to keep my cool in the Bhoolabyrinth, and *you* did,' said Zarpa quietly. 'We all only get by with a little help from our friends.'

Zvala flushed. 'Sorry, just being a swollen-headed sillykoof as always.' She scratched away at her papyrus pad diligently, filling in the words of the riddle.

Five dinglings later, when Tufan walked in, spiking his wet hair with his fingers and reeking of Max Deo, Zvala was ready.

'In the Drip-Trip Cave, by the Shimrflies' glow
The Venompires will hunt you, high and low
There hangs the key that sets the Citrines free
In the deep deep dark of Chuk R'Vue Three.'

'As you can see, Taranaut Tufan,' she ended haughtily, 'we will not be needing your services today.'

Tufan grabbed a fistful of golden solaberries from a bowl and crammed them into his mouth. 'Simple, wasn't it?' he mumbled. 'Everything always is, once you've eat . . . Hey!'

Zvala had sprung to her feet, grabbed a firm red sebapple, and was taking careful aim. 'Just *saying*,' chuckled Tufan, ducking neatly as the sebapple crashed into the wall above him.

Thirteen

'Hang them up by their wrists in the dungeons!' raged Ograzur Dusht. 'Give them nothing but annakki water, *once* a day. Yes, *all* of them, including the spineless Captain!'

Two Demazurs bowed and left to carry out his bidding, relieved that they hadn't been part of the regiment that had faced the horror of the Muggarosaur. Mithyakins they could handle, even superhero ones, but Muggarosaurs were a different kettle of meenmaach altogether.

Dusht turned to the three with him. 'You three are hereby promoted to the rank of Captain,' he said. The new Captains fell to their knees slavishly, scraping the ground before Dusht with their foreheads.

'You!' Dusht pointed to the one in the middle, cringing a little inside that he could not even remember the mithyaka's name. He wasn't usually like this—he had always prided himself on his memory, but he had recruited so many mithyakos recently that it was impossible to keep track any more. 'Take your regiment and head to the Drip-Trip Cave on CRV3. Keep guard at the exit of the cavern.' The Demazur nodded.

'You!' he pointed to another one. 'Wait at the main exit of the cave with your men and trap the brats there if they ever get out. And you,' he said to the third, 'stand by at CRV3 and wait for further orders. But before you leave,' Dusht pulled his whip off the wall, sending a little makdiboochi scuttling hastily away, 'take a look at this beauty. Fail in this mission, and you will get to know her more intimately than you desire, when I personally strip the skin off your backs with a centillion lashes.'

The Captains swallowed. 'We will not fail you, Ograzur! *Harharadusht!*'

In another part of XadYuntra, a group of mithyakos sat up suddenly as Raaksh appeared in their midst.

'I managed to get a good perch on the wall of the War Room,' he panted. 'Dusht's army is headed for a place called the Drip-Trip Cave—that's where the brats are going next.'

'There's no time to waste, then,' Hidim Bi got to her aching feet. 'Paapi, look through the archives for images of the cave, so you three can stelliport there with your soldiers. I will stay here, at mission control. Go, go, go!'

'It all looks very peaceful from here,' said Zarpa doubtfully, peering into the darkness of the Drip Trip Cave. 'It was easy getting here, we haven't met any creepy mithyakos . . .'

'. . . and my lungs do seem to be adapting surprisingly well to the lack of oxdrogen here,' added Tufan happily. 'But it *is* hot!'

'*Phew*, yes!' Zvala mopped her forehead with a damp handkerchief and pulled at her clothes. They clung stubbornly to her, wet with sweat. 'Zarpa, did you look up Drip Trip Cave last 'nite?'

'Yes, I did,' said Zarpa, pulling out a map. 'The Drip Trip cave is called that because the main cavern—here, right at the centre—is full of stalacdrips—mineral stuff that drips from the ceiling and solidifies, and stalagtrips—mineral stuff that oozes from the floor and builds up into solid fingers that trip you up.'

'What about the Venompires?'

'Ah yes, the Venompires,' Zarpa said slowly. 'Hazillions of them roost inside the main cavern, hanging upside down from their rocky perches. They are khoonsuckers that prey on rodents and other small creatures, not mithyakos. If they get their fangs into you, however, your nerves go into instant paralysis, putting you out of commission for a couple of octolls.' Zvala let out a wail. '*But*,' continued Zarpa, 'they are very shy, and are not known to attack mithyakos unprovoked.'

'Oh well, I'm sure *someone* has plenty of provocation planned,' said Tufan, his eyes flashing, 'but nothing that the Taranauts cannot deal with. Come on, guys, we have exactly six dings left to the end of the octoll.'

Half a ding later, pouring with sweat, the Taranauts rounded the corner to the centre of the Drip Trip Cave and into the main cavern, and stood there, gasping in wonder. Standing tall—and hanging low—were hazillions of 'drips and 'trips, glowing a soft translucent gold in the twinkling light of mazillions of shimrflies. Venompires hung everywhere, their heads tucked under their wings, asleep. Suspended by a string from the central 'drip, low enough for the Taranauts to reach, was a papyrus scroll.

Take off your Rayviators, said Zvala. *You can see better without them here.*

Right, said Zarpa. *Very, very carefully now.* They began to tiptoe, in single file, towards the scroll.

Ten dinglings later, they were there. *This was almost too easy,* Tufan reached for the scroll and tugged hard.

With a sudden, ear-spliiting *CRRRRAACKKKK!*, the whole 'drip came loose from the ceiling and began to fall, its sharp point heading straight for Tufan's foot! Yelping with alarm, Tufan tore away the scroll and leapt out of the way. The 'drip hit the floor of the cave with a thud that sent a shudder around the cave, loosening the shimrfly nests and setting fine cracks racing through the more delicate 'drips. The sound of splintering resounded through the cavern as other 'drips began to break off and tumble down. Screeching ferociously at being disturbed, hazillions of venompires came alive and began to swoop through the cave in furious arcs, determined to punish the culprits!

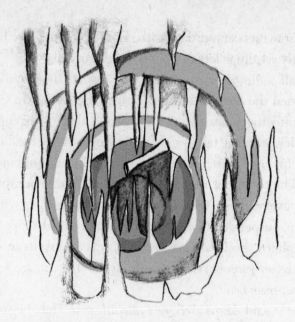

Run! yelled Zarpa. *The exit is over to the left!*

In one of the dark passages surrounded the cavern, Shurpa gave her brother a thumbs up. 'Now, Raaksh! Dusht's men are just beyond that exit.'

Raaksh nodded. The next instant, another venompire, larger than the others, had joined the flock in the cavern. It headed straight for Tufan, dipping suddenly to snatch the scroll from his fingers. Then it glided off towards the cavern exit.

'Hey!' cried Tufan, struggling to pull out the 'drip that had pinned his trouser leg to the ground. 'Come back here! Team, that venompire has our scroll. Follow him!'

An angry screeching began among the venompires at the sight and smell of the new creature. Forgetting about the Taranauts, they gave chase, determined to drive the interloper out. A dingling later, the cavern echoed with screams of fear and agony as the venompires crashed into the unsuspecting group of soldiers outside and panicked, sinking their fangs into them. As his mithyakas fell like ninepins around him, paralyzed, the Captain lost his nerve. 'Retreat!' he yelled. 'Let the others take care of the brats!'

A little baffled by the turn of events, but still completely focused on the venompire that held their scroll, the Taranauts raced through the melee. Raaksh, who had

explored the cave thoroughly and discovered a couple of other exits, led them away from the main exit, where he knew Dusht's men waited, and towards one where Shurpa and Paapi crouched, expectant and ready.

But suddenly, the plot changed once again. Screeching mightily, yet *another* venompire came swooping out of one of the dark passages, its furry wings gleaming blue-black and dull gold. It attacked Raaksh mercilessly, pinning him against the cave wall with its talons, then plunged its fangs into him before he had time to react. Raaksh fell, turning back into his normal shape as he hit the ground.

A Morphoroop! gasped Zvala. *It's one of the Ograzurs we met at Shawksar Ovar.*

Whatever, said Tufan, still focused on the new venompire, which had turned around and was heading in a completely different direction, the scroll clutched firmly in its mouth. *Come on—we've got to get our riddle back!*

Ten dinglings later, the blue-black venompire sped out of the Drip Trip Cave through an unguarded exit and disappeared. Tufan raced after him.

We've lost him! cried Zarpa. *What do we do now?* She sank to the ground outside, exhausted.

We solve the riddle, I guess. Tufan brandished the scroll, looking bemused. *For some reason, the venompire decided to leave this behind.*

Fourteen

Let's head to the nearest Litechowk! said Zvala urgently, copying a look at Zarpa's dingdial. *Only one ding to go.*

Only a few dim arcalamps burned at the Litechowk they sped into ten dinglings later, but there was enough light to read by.

TURN TURN THE THE TOP BE BE BE BE SPIN 2 O'DING

'That's *it*?' Tufan gawked at it. 'What does it mean?'

'We need to spin a top of some kind by 2 o' ding? But it's already 31 o'ding!' Zarpa's voice rose hysterically. 'And why does it say the same words again and again?'

Zvala had been staring at the scroll without comment. 'The repetition is deliberate,' she said. 'It means something. So "TURN TURN" will mean "two turn" or "turn again" or "re-turn". . . . *Return*! That's it!'

'That means "THE THE" could mean "Re-the", "the again", "two the" . . . *to the*,' yelled Tufan. *'Return to the . . . ,'* he looked at the scroll again, *'Return to the top!'*

'Before 2 o'ding?' Zarpa blanched. 'That means we have missed our deadline!'

'Stop jumping to conclusions, Captain,' snapped Zvala. 'There's more. "BE BE BE BE" is "four be" or ...'

'Be four?' ventured Zarpa in a small voice.

'*Yes*! Before!' squealed Zvala. 'Before when, though? Tufan, what's another word for "Spin"?'

'Turn? Twist? Flick? *Ummm* . . . flip?'

'*Fliptime*!' Zvala yelled triumphantly. '2 o' ding is a time. *'Return to the top before fliptime'*! That's all! Easy-peasy!'

'Is it really?' said Zarpa, glancing nervously at her dingdial. 'We are on CRV3, remember? We can only go up by three flights of Infinite Steepstairs—and even I can't cover that distance in half a ding. Plus, I'm sure Shaap Azur has them all heavily guarded.'

'Add to that a couple of other problems that have suddenly made their appearance,' Tufan muttered, looking fearfully behind Zvala. *'Run, team!'*

Two groups of armed Downsiders were rushing into the Litechowk, heading straight for the Taranauts. The third regiment of Dusht's army roared down one passage leading to the Litechowk, a ragtag bunch led by Ograzur Paapi came thundering down another.

Zarpa looked around her, thinking fast. *Down the low narrow passage to the right, team. We'll fit in there all right, but I doubt many of these guys will. Follow me!*

The three of them ducked into the narrow opening and pounded down the passage. Behind them, their two sets of pursuers clashed at the entrance of the passage, each determined to be the only ones to go after the Taranauts. Stunsabres clanged and tranqslugs flew as a full-scale battle broke out in the Litechowk.

Tufan began to laugh. *Good thinking, Captain! We've lost them for the moment!*

We seem to have two different sets of mithyakos after us now, said Zarpa. *Double trouble.*

Or not, said Tufan. *Seems to me like the opposition is now split down the middle. Which can only be good for us.*

If you two are quite done nattering on back there, Zvala called over her shoulder, *we still have the problem of getting back to the surface in the next ten . . .*

She stopped suddenly as she tumbled out of the dark passage and into the bottom of a deep ventilation shaft. *Ohhhh, this feels gooood.* The three of them paused, taking in deep lungfuls of fresh cool air.

'It's the Tarabrats! Get them!' The second regiment of Dusht's mithyakas emerged into the ventilation shaft. They had waited in vain for the Taranauts at the main exit of the Cave, and were now making their reluctant way home, wondering what terrible punishment awaited there.

Not again! groaned Zvala.

'Zvala, hold them!' Zarpa took charge. 'There's enough oxdrogen here to get your fire going. Tufan, now would be a good time to see what Achmentor Vak's bubblechews can do!'

Delighted to be Fully Functional Firegirl again, Zvala
let fly a burst of heat at the oncoming soldiers. Tufan
popped all six pieces of bubblechew into his mouth,
and began to work his jaws.

I can't hold them off much longer, called Zvala, five
dinglings later. *There are too many of them!*

You won't have to, said Zarpa. *Turn around!*

Zvala turned, and gasped. Tufan stood on tiptoe in
the centre of the shaft, arms akimbo, head thrown back.
Out of his pursed lips grew the biggest, shiniest, golden
bubble she had ever seen. As she stared, Tufan teetered a
little, about to be carried away!

Grab my arms, both of you! Hold me down for a little longer!
Zvala and Zarpa ran to Tufan. The bubble grew bigger and
bigger, its skin getting thinner and shinier.

'Stop them!' cried the Captain. 'They're up to
something!' The soldiers rushed towards the Taranauts.

Hold tight! yelled Tufan. *Up, up and away!*

As the soldiers watched, their faces foolish and

uncomprehending, the giant golden bubble rose into the air, trailing its precious cargo securely behind it. It sailed up the long, long ventilation shaft, climbing steadily past CRV2 and CRV1 until it burst out of the top, shining triumphantly. Instantly, four golden suns zipped into the sky, flooding the pockmarked surface of Shimr with glorious Citrinelite.

'Inhale, Tufan, inhale the air out of the bubble!' A familiar voice cautioned from the surface. Tufan inhaled. The bubble grew smaller and smaller, and began to drop gently towards the ground, towards where a merry-eyed mithyaka in an indigo-gold braid stood, next to a bent little Shimrkos whose grin took up more than half his face.

'Bravo, mithyakins!' said Treepli, his voice shaking with emotion. The strong limbulimey scent of Max Deo filled the air. 'Come back and see us soon in the deep, deep dark-dark-dark.'

'We will, Treepli,' promised Zvala. 'And we will talk to the Emperaza and Ms Shuk Tee about how things are here. Expect some major changes soon. Starting, imhaho,' her face grew black as a thundercloud, 'with a new, improved Maraza.'

'Quickly, hold hands, everyone,' Zub stretched out his hands. 'Close your eyes. "See" the Tower Room on Kay Laas! "See" the 24 Tarasuns in the sky! Let's go-o-o!'

Fifteen

'How does Shimr look now, Ms Shuk Tee?' The Taranauts had just walked in the Tower Room, well-rested and fed, to find Shuk Tee staring out at the north-eastern sky, where the Citrines blazed in all their former glory.

Shuk Tee turned. Her face glowed as if someone had lit an arcalamp inside it, and she looked as she had done an octoll ago, when she had first spoken to them about Shimr. 'Thank you,' she said simply. 'Thank you for the Citrines.'

Zvala cleared her throat. 'It's your dad you should thank, Ms Shuk Tee,' she said hesitantly. 'It was the gifts he gave us that helped us succeed on this mission.'

Shuk Tee's eyebrows shot up in surprise, and the glow disappeared. 'I didn't know you had met him, or that . . . or that he had *helped* you . . .'

There was an awkward silence. Then Zarpa spoke.

'There may be other things about him you don't know, Ms Shuk Tee,' she said quietly. 'Maybe if you let him explain . . .'

A flash of anger jumped into Shuk Tee's face. Zarpa flinched, expecting her to lash out, but she simply turned towards the window again, looking towards Shimr.

'He is very old now,' Tufan said. 'And he really wants to see you again.'

Shuk Tee did not respond. The last two octolls had been an emotional rollercoaster, and she had slacked off on her responsibilities. The traitor who had taken the Marani of Glo's messages to Achmentor Aaq was still on the loose in Zum Skar. The toughest challenges the Taranauts would face still lay ahead, and she needed to ensure that they got all the help they needed. With only eight Tarasuns left to rescue, the Great Zamara loomed ever closer. But . . . surely, she could still squeeze a few dings out, for herself?

She turned away from the window, and took the Taranauts' hands in hers. 'Maybe I *will* go and see him,' she said. 'Maybe it's time to go home.'

Zarpa smiled. 'We'll be right here waiting for you when you return, Ms Shuk Tee,' she promised.